Animal Stories

Cover illustrated by Angela Keoghan

Illustrated by Xuan Le, Hannah Tolson, Mei Matsuoka, Hannah Peck,
Tiziana Longo, Victoria Assanelli, Mar Ferrero, Julianna Swaney,
Alessandra Psacharopulo, Libby Burns, Galia Bernstein, Iris Deppe,
Neesha Hudson, Katie Wilson, Claire McElfatrick, and Jenny Løvlie.

Selected stories retold by
Anne Rooney, Mandy Archer, Catherine Allison, Lilly Holland,
Etta Saunders, Karen Ball, and Claire Sipi.

Every effort has been made to
acknowledge the contributors of this book.
If we have made any errors, we will be pleased
to rectify them in future editions.

Created 2018 by Parragon Books, Ltd.
Copyright © 2019 Cottage Door Press, LLC
5005 Newport Drive, Rolling Meadows, Illinois 60008
All Rights Reserved

ISBN 978-1-68052-468-0

Cottage Door Press® and the Cottage Door Press® logo
are registered trademarks of Cottage Door Press, LLC.

Animal Stories

cottage door press

Contents
Stories and Fables

The Ugly Duckling   8

The Tortoise and the Hare   14

The Three Little Pigs   20

The Crow and the Pitcher   26

The Frogs Who Wanted a King   30

Goldilocks and the Three Bears   36

The Cat That Walked by Himself   42

The Wolf in Sheep's Clothing   50

The Little Red Hen   56

Wild Swans   62

The Lion and the Mouse   70

The Frog Prince   78

Puss in Boots   86

The Nightingale   92

The Three Billy Goats Gruff   100

How the Leopard Got His Spots   106

The Peacock and the Crane   112

The Wolf and the Seven Little Kids   118

The Town Mouse and the Country Mouse   124

The Dog and His Reflection   132

Chicken Little   138

The Ant and the Grasshopper   146

The Rooster and the Fox   152

The Vain Crow   158

Songs and Rhymes

Old Mother Goose	164
Itsy Bitsy Spider	166
Ride a Cock-Horse	167
Five Little Ducks	168
Sing a Song of Sixpence	170
The Animals Went in Two by Two	172
B-I-N-G-O	176
This Little Piggy	178
Hickety Pickety	179
Goosey Goosey Gander	180
Baa, Baa, Black Sheep	181
Mary Had a Little Lamb	182
Hey Diddle Diddle	184
Little Bo-Peep	186
Pussycat, Pussycat	187
Old MacDonald Had a Farm	188

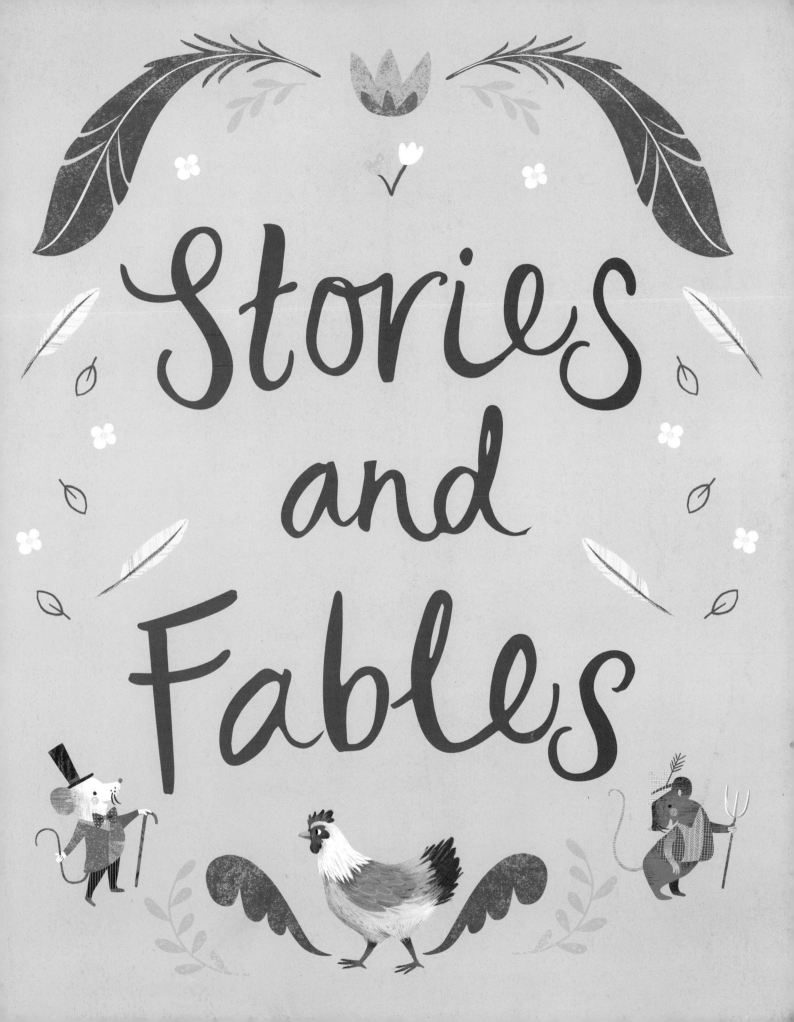

Stories and Fables

The Ugly Duckling

Once upon a time, a proud and excited duck was waiting for her eggs to hatch. "Soon I will have seven beautiful ducklings," she told anyone who would listen.

It wasn't long before she heard a **CRACK!** And one fluffy yellow duckling popped her little head out of the shell.

"She's perfect!" Mother Duck exclaimed. Soon, there was another … and then another … until she had six beautiful little ducklings, drying their fluffy yellow wings in the spring air.

"Just one egg left," quacked Mother Duck, "and it's a big one!" But for quite a while, nothing happened. Mother Duck was starting to worry when, at last, the big egg began to hatch.

Tap, tap, tap! Out came a bumpy beak.

Crack, crack, crack! Out popped a curious head.

Crunch, crunch, crunch! Out came the last duckling.

"Oh, my!" said Mother Duck. "Isn't he … different!"

The last duckling did look strange. He was bigger than the other ducklings and his feathers weren't lovely and yellow, but gray.

"That's all right," said Mother Duck. "You're my extra special little duckling. Now come on into the water," she said to her tiny hatchlings. "You must learn to swim right away."

One by one, the ducklings hopped into the water, landing with a little plop. But the ugly duckling fell over his big feet and landed in the water with a great big **SPLASH!** The other ducklings laughed at their clumsy brother.

"Now, my little ones," said Mother Duck, "stick together and stay behind me!"

Back at the nest, the ducklings practiced their quacking.

"Repeat after me," said their mother. "Quack, quack, quackety-quack!"

"Quack, quack, quackety-quack!" repeated the ducklings, all except for one.

"Honk! Honk!" called the ugly duckling. However much he tried, he couldn't quack like his brothers and sisters.

"Now, now," soothed Mother Duck. "I'm sure you'll get the hang of it soon enough."

The other ducklings quacked with laughter, and the ugly duckling hung his head in shame. "Nobody likes me," he thought. "I'll never fit in."

The next day, Mother Duck took her little ones to the river. The ducklings waddled happily behind her in pairs, and left the ugly duckling at the back to wander alone.

He watched as wild geese came swooping down and landed on the river nearby.

"What kind of a bird are you?" asked one goose, rather rudely.

"I'm a duckling," said the ugly duckling. "My family is right there... oh." Mother Duck and his brothers and sisters had kept waddling, and were now far away in the distance.

The geese felt sorry for the ugly duckling. "Come with us," they said. "It's a big wide world, and there's so much to see!"

"No, thank you," replied the ugly duckling. "I belong with my family." And he waddled off quickly to catch up.

As the days passed, the other ducklings began to tease their ugly brother when their mother wasn't listening.

"Just look at his dull feathers," said his sister, admiring her own reflection in the water. "He's so ugly!"

The ugly duckling swam away and looked at his reflection. "I am ugly," he thought. "I don't look the same as them."

Feeling sad and lonely, he swam down the river and didn't stop until he'd reached a place he had never seen before. "I'll be better off staying here by myself," he decided.

Summer turned to autumn. The sky became cloudy and the river murky. All the while the ugly duckling swam alone in his quiet part of the river.

Snow fell heavily that winter, and the ugly duckling was cold and lonely. The river froze solid. "At least I can't see my ugly reflection anymore," he thought to himself.

Spring arrived at last, and the ice thawed. New visitors arrived on the river. The ugly duckling watched nervously as some magnificent white birds swam toward him.

"You're very beautiful ducks," he told them.

"Why, we're not ducks," laughed the elegant creatures. "We're swans — just like you!"

The ugly duckling didn't know what they meant. For the first time that spring he looked at his reflection in the river ... and was surprised to see beautiful white feathers and an elegant long neck.

"Is that really me?" he asked. He had changed so much!

"Of course," they said. "You are a truly handsome swan. Would you like to join us?"

The young swan agreed, overjoyed to have friends at last.

As he glided gracefully up the river, he swam past a family of ducks. Mother Duck recognized her ugly duckling right away. "I always knew he was special," she said, gazing at him proudly.

The beautiful young swan ruffled his magnificent white feathers and held his elegant head high. He finally felt as though he belonged.

The Tortoise and the Hare

The hare and the tortoise were neighbors. Hare was always in a hurry, rushing from one important task to another.

He was so fast and busy that sometimes he could barely remember where he was going. Tortoise, on the other hand, plodded steadily along. He didn't go to many different places in a day, but he always got to where he needed to be.

One day, Tortoise was walking slowly along the road when Hare sped past him. Hare looked over his shoulder and called out, "Hurry up, Tortoise — you'll never get there!"

"I will," Tortoise said calmly, "I will. Slow, but steady."

Hare turned back and ran around Tortoise three times, laughing. Then he ran on.

Half an hour later, Hare came back. Tortoise was still going in the same direction, and he hadn't gotten very far.

"You're so slow!" Hare said. "How do you ever get anywhere?"

"Look," Tortoise said. "One step at a time. One foot after the other. Slow, but steady."

"You're hopeless!" Hare said. "It will take you all day just to get to the end of the road!"

At last, Tortoise was too cross to ignore Hare any longer.

"I get everywhere I want to go!" he said. "And if you don't believe me, I'll challenge you to a race. You can pick the route, the day, and the time."

Hare laughed until he fell over. He rolled around on the ground, tears running along his whiskers.

"A race?" he gasped. "Between you and me? That's ridiculous! You don't stand a chance."

"Are you scared?" Tortoise asked. "Because if not, let's do it."

15

Hare could hardly stop laughing, but they arranged the race for the next day and asked Fox to judge it. They would start from an old oak tree and race all the way to the river.

Tortoise set out early that evening so that he would be at the start line on time in the morning.

Hare went home for a long sleep and got up late. He ran to the oak tree and found Tortoise ready and waiting. All the other animals had come out to watch.

"Fox is waiting for you at the river," Bear said. "We can start whenever you're ready."

Hare and Tortoise got into position.

"On your marks," said Tortoise.

"Get set," said Hare.

"Go!" shouted all the animals.

And off went the tortoise and the hare.

Hare sprinted ahead, bounding along the path. Tortoise lifted one foot, and put it down. Then he lifted the other foot, and put it down. Slowly, slowly. By the time Tortoise reached the first bush, Hare was a tiny spot in the distance. By the time he reached the second bush, Hare was nowhere to be seen.

After a few minutes, Hare could see the river ahead. He paused and looked around. He couldn't see Tortoise at all.

"He is so slow!" he laughed to himself. "He won't be here for hours. I might as well have a rest." So Hare sat down under a tree not far from the finish line. The sun was warm, and the lazy buzz of bees visiting the flowers around him was soothing. Soon Hare dozed off.

Back along the path, Tortoise kept on, slow but steady, one step at a time, one foot after the other.

After an hour, Hare woke up and peered into the distance. He could just see Tortoise coming toward him, slow but steady, and still far away.

"He's so slow!" Hare said to himself. "He won't be here for hours. I might as well go back to sleep." And that's just what he did.

Tortoise kept on, slow but steady, his heavy shell wobbling along the path. Hare slept on in the hot sun.

When Hare woke up, he couldn't see Tortoise anywhere.

"Where has he gone?" he said. "He won't be here for hours, I'm sure. I could just go back to sleep." But it was late afternoon and the sun was low in the sky. "I'm sick of this race," he said to himself. "I should finish so I can go home and nap in my own bed." And he sprang up and ran as fast as he could to the finish line.

Tortoise was waiting for him by the river.

"Where have you been?" asked Tortoise. "I've been here for hours. You are so slow!"

Hare tried to explain, but neither Tortoise nor Fox would listen.

"But I'm faster!" Hare complained. "It's not fair!"

"The rules were simple," Fox said. "Tortoise won."

"The race was to get here first," Tortoise smiled, "not to run fastest. Slow and steady wins the race!" And slowly, steadily, he turned around to begin his journey home.

The Three Little Pigs

Once upon a time, three little pigs lived with their mother. As they grew bigger, their small house became too crowded. At last, Mother Pig decided to send her three children off into the world to seek their fortunes.

"Be careful," she said. "And watch out for the big, bad wolf. You will need to build strong houses to keep him out."

The pigs set off happily. After a short time, the first little pig met a farmer pulling a cartload of straw.

"Please may I have some straw to build a house?" the little pig asked. He was tired, and didn't want to walk any farther.

"Certainly," the farmer said, "but it won't make a very strong house."

The little pig didn't listen. He took the bundles of straw and stacked them up to make a house. When it was finished, he went inside for a rest.

Soon, the big, bad wolf came down the road. He hadn't eaten all day. When he saw the new house of straw, his tummy rumbled and he licked his lips.

"What do we have here?" he said to himself.

He peeked in through the window and saw the little pig.

"Little pig, little pig, let me come in," he growled.

"No way!" the pig shouted nervously. "Not by the hairs on my chinny-chin-chin!"

"Well, this straw doesn't look very strong," the wolf said. "I'll **huff**, and I'll **puff**, and I'll **blow** your house down!"

So he huffed and he puffed, and it wasn't long before the straw house tumbled down, down, down. Straw flew everywhere, and the little pig ran away as fast as his legs would carry him.

The second little pig walked a little farther. At last, he came across a woodcutter with a pile of sticks. "Please could I have some sticks to build a house?" the little pig asked.

"Certainly," said the woodcutter. "Take as many as you like, but they won't make a very strong house."

The second little pig didn't listen. He picked up all the sticks he could carry and took them to a clearing. He piled them up to make a cozy house. When it was finished, he went inside and settled down with a cup of coffee.

The big, bad wolf was cross and hungry. When he saw the house of sticks, his tummy grumbled and he licked his lips.

"Well, well, well," he said to himself. "Another little pig!"

He pushed his nose against the door.

"Little pig, little pig, let me come in," he growled.

"No way!" the second little pig shouted. "Not by the hairs on my chinny-chin-chin!"

"Well, these sticks don't look very strong," the wolf said. "I'll **huff**, and I'll **puff**, and I'll **blow** your house down!"

And so he huffed and he puffed, and it wasn't long before the wood house crashed down, down, down. Sticks tumbled to the ground, and the little pig ran away as fast as he could.

The third little pig walked farther still, until he saw a builder with a pile of bricks. The builder was just finishing work.

"Please could I have some bricks to build a little house?" the third little pig asked.

"Certainly," the builder said. "Those are left over. Take as many as you want."

So the third little pig carried the bricks away and built a beautiful house. When he had finished, he went inside, put a pot of water on the fire, and started to make some soup.

After a while, his two brothers came running up the path.

"Let us in!" they shouted. "There's a big, bad wolf coming!" The third little pig quickly let them in. They locked and bolted the door and sat down to wait.

Before long, the big, bad wolf came huffing and puffing up the path. When he saw the new brick house, his tummy rumbled and grumbled and he licked his lips.

"Dinner at last!" he said to himself. "Yum, yum, yum!"

He knocked hard on the door. "Little pigs, little pigs, let me come in!" he roared.

"No way!" the third little pig shouted. "Not by the hairs on our chinny-chin-chins!"

"Well, then," the wolf said, "I'll **huff**, and I'll **puff**, and I'll **blow** your house down!"

And so he huffed and he puffed, and he huffed and he puffed ... but the brick house stood firm.

The wolf looked up and saw the chimney. He climbed onto the roof, and down the chimney he went — straight into the pot of hot soup.

"OOWWWWWEEEEE!"

He jumped out of the pot and ran yowling and howling, out into the cool night. The big, bad wolf ran up the path, over the hills, and far away, never to be seen again.

The three little pigs lived happily ever after, all together in the strong brick house.

The Crow and the Pitcher

It was a scorching summer's day in the meadow, and Crow sat in his favorite oak tree. Usually a cooling breeze swayed the leaves around him, but today there was no breeze.

Crow felt as though his black feathers were melting in the unbearable heat. He tried to swallow, but his throat was scratchy and dry.

He flew down to a large rock beside the stream, and as he landed he knocked a pebble into the water. It hit the stream with a satisfying plop, and cool water splashed his feet. Crow was just about to dip his beak into the water, when there was a sudden whooshing sound from above.

A hawk was zooming through the air toward him, its hooked beak gleaming menacingly.

Crow flapped his wings furiously and managed to leap out of the way just in time.

"I'll get you next time!" the hawk called after Crow, as he hastily flew back to his oak tree to hide.

What could he do now? He was still so thirsty, but he wasn't going near that stream again — not while the hawk was there. His mom's voice rang in his ears:

"There's no problem you can't solve, if you just take the time to think about it."

"Think, Crow, think!" he told himself. Maybe the farmhouse would hold some answers.

When Crow landed in the farmhouse garden, he spotted a kitten lapping up water from a saucer. "Aha!" he whispered.

But the kitten drank every last drop and wandered into the cool shade of the farmhouse.

Crow glanced around in despair … then he spotted a tall pitcher standing on a table. Crow flew over and peered inside the pitcher. It was tall and narrow, and halfway down he could see the glint of — water!

The crow poked his beak inside the pitcher and stuck out his tongue. But no matter how hard he tried, he couldn't reach the water. He sank back on his clawed feet and gave a little sob.

Just then, there was a crunch of pebbles as the farm dog ran out into the yard.

Pebbles! That was it! He flew down and picked up a pebble, then dropped it into the pitcher. **Clunk!** He peered inside. The water had risen. Not by much, but it was a start.

Crow flew back and forth with pebbles to drop into the pitcher.

With each one, the water started
to rise and rise until it brimmed at the
pitcher's rim. "Success!" the crow cried as he
gulped down a long, glorious drink at last.

Crow drank until his feathers had cooled, then he
flew back home to his favorite branch in the oak tree.
The hawk was gone.

As Crow's feet landed on the rough bark, he
remembered his mother's voice again.

"There's no problem you can't solve," she said,
"if you just take the time to think about it."

The Frogs Who
Wanted a King

It was another noisy day at the pond. The morning air was filled with the sound of angry croaking, and the clear blue water was rough with ripples and waves. The frogs were quarreling again.

All over the pond, they were pushing and shoving, puffing up their chests, and shouting at the tops of their voices. They were arguing about everything: who could sit on which lily pad, who had the most warts, and, most of all, who could croak the loudest. The noise was deafening.

One old green frog, who was trying to get some sleep under a rock, covered his ears, but he could still hear everything.

Exasperated, he took a deep breath and shouted,

"BE QUIET!" in a voice so loud that all the other frogs stopped croaking at once in surprise.

"Listen, everyone," said the old frog. "We must stop all this arguing. It's horrible to listen to, and it never ends. There must be another way to settle our quarrels."

There was silence on the pond.

"I have an idea," he said. "What if we ask Zeus to choose a king for us? That king could solve all our arguments."

The other frogs thought this was a great plan and croaked in agreement.

"I'm going to see Zeus right away," said the old frog. "Who's coming with me?"

The great god Zeus lived high up on Mount Olympus, in a palace in the clouds. When the frogs arrived, he was sitting on his cloudy throne, eating grapes from a huge golden bowl.

"Your majesty," said the old frog politely, "we frogs cannot live in peace together, and we need someone to lead us. Please, can you find us a king?"

"Hmm," said Zeus, looking down at the frog. "What kind of king are you looking for?"

"Someone who is a good listener," called out a bold young frog.

"And someone we can look up to," added another.

Zeus chuckled. "These frogs have no idea what it's like to have a king. Let's see if they like the one I choose for them," he thought.

"Go back to your pond at once," he told them, "and I will send you a king."

The frogs hopped home to their pond and waited. Suddenly, there was a flash of light and a gust of wind, and a large wooden log landed in the water with a splash.

At first, the frogs were frightened, but when the water was calm again, they were excited. They had a king!

"Amazing!" they croaked. "Look how strong he is and how quietly he listens."

One by one, the frogs approached the log and politely asked for help to solve their disagreement. The log, of course, said nothing.

It wasn't long before the frogs gave up and started sitting on their "king" instead, as if he was just an ordinary log.

The frogs visited Zeus again.

"Your majesty," began the old frog politely, "thank you for the king you sent us, but unfortunately, he wasn't quite what we wanted. Please, can you send us a different one, who answers when we speak to him and doesn't just sit around all day long?"

Zeus smiled to himself, but he agreed to send them another king.

The frogs went back to their pond, and this time Zeus sent a large brown eel in a flash of light.

As first, the frogs were delighted. The eel was friendly and talkative, not silent at all like the log. He seemed to be the perfect king.

But after a while, they realized that he was actually *too* friendly and talkative. Once he started giving his advice, it was impossible to keep him from talking!

The frogs went back to Zeus a third time. The god was resting and was very irritated to see them again.

"Let me guess … you want a different king?" he asked them crossly. "I will send you another one. But this will be your last."

The frogs went home and waited for their new king. They were excited. What would he be like? Strong and friendly but not too talkative, they hoped, and someone they could look up to.

They didn't have to wait very long. With a blinding flash of light and an icy gust of wind, a large gray heron appeared.

All the frogs were terrified because they knew that herons ate frogs.

The heron's beady eyes glinted, his sharp beak snapped, he swooped low over the water, and the frogs ran for their lives. They hid in the mud, under the rocks, and anywhere else they could find, and they never showed their faces on the surface of the pond again.

From then on, they tried very hard to solve their disagreements themselves!

Goldilocks and the Three Bears

Once upon a time, there was a little girl named Goldilocks, who had beautiful golden hair. She lived in a pretty house right at the edge of the forest. Each morning, she liked to play outside before breakfast, gathering flowers and looking at the animals who lived in the trees.

One day, she strayed farther than usual. She skipped happily along the forest path, chasing butterflies, until she was far from home and very hungry.

Just as she was thinking that it would take a long time to walk back for breakfast, a delicious smell wafted through the woods. She followed it all the way to a little cottage.

"I wonder who lives here?" Goldilocks said to herself. "Perhaps they would share their breakfast with me?" She knocked on the door, but there was no answer.

As Goldilocks pushed gently on the door, it swung open. The house inside was cozy and inviting. Even though she knew she shouldn't, Goldilocks stepped inside.

The delicious smell was coming from three bowls of steaming porridge on the table. There was a great big bowl, a medium-sized bowl, and a teeny-tiny bowl. Goldilocks was so hungry that—even though she knew she shouldn't—she tasted the porridge in the biggest bowl.

"Ow!" she cried. "This porridge is too hot!"

Next, she tasted the porridge in the medium-sized bowl. "Yuck!" she said. "This porridge is much too cold!"

So finally, she tried the porridge in the teeny-tiny bowl. "Yum!" Goldilocks said. "This porridge is just right!" And she ate it all up.

With her tummy nice and full, Goldilocks decided to take a rest before she set out for home. She looked around the room for somewhere to sit. There were three chairs: a great big chair, a medium-sized chair, and a teeny-tiny chair.

She climbed onto the great big chair. "This chair is much too high," she said.

Next, she tried the medium-sized chair, but she sank deep into the cushions. "No," she said, "this chair is much too squashy."

So she sat on the teeny-tiny chair. "This chair is just right!" she said, settling in.

But Goldilocks was very full of porridge and too heavy for the teeny-tiny chair. It **squeaked** and **creaked**. It **creaked** and **cracked**.

Then **CRASH!** It broke into teeny-tiny pieces, and Goldilocks fell to the floor.

"Well, that wasn't a very good chair!" she said crossly.

Then, even though she knew she shouldn't, she went to look upstairs.

CRASHHH!

In the bedroom were three beds. A great big bed, a medium-sized bed, and a teeny-tiny bed.

She tried to lie down on the great big bed, but it wasn't at all comfy. "This bed is too hard and lumpy," she grumbled.

Then Goldilocks lay down on the medium-sized bed, but that was no better. "This bed is too soft and squishy," she mumbled. And so, at last, she snuggled down in the teeny-tiny bed.

"This bed is just right!" she said, and fell fast asleep.

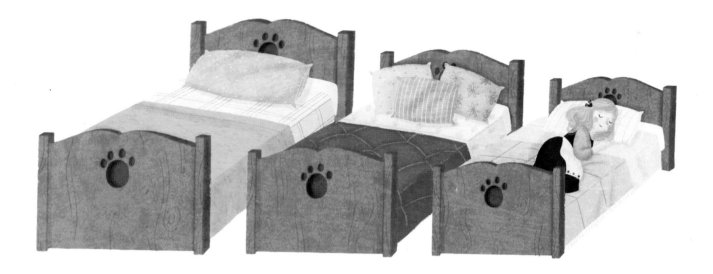

What Goldilocks didn't know, was that right at that very moment three brown bears were on their way to the house. There was a great big daddy bear, a medium-sized mommy bear, and a teeny-tiny baby bear.

The three bears lived in that little cottage. They had made their porridge that very morning and gone out for a walk in the woods while it cooled down. At last, they decided to go home for their breakfast.

"Why is the front door open?" Daddy Bear said, in his deep, gruff voice.

"Why are there footprints on the floor?" Mommy Bear said, in her soft, low voice.

"Why is there a funny smell in here?" Baby Bear said, in his teeny-tiny voice.

They went over to the table, and Daddy Bear looked in his breakfast bowl. "Someone's been eating my porridge!" he growled.

Mommy Bear looked in her bowl. "Someone's been eating *my* porridge!" she exclaimed.

Baby Bear looked in his bowl. "Someone's been eating *my* porridge — and they've eaten it all up!" he cried.

Daddy Bear stomped over to his chair. "Someone's been sitting in my chair!" he growled. "There's a long hair on it!"

"Someone's been sitting in *my* chair!" Mommy Bear exclaimed. "The cushions are all squashed!"

Baby Bear looked at his chair. "Someone's been sitting in my chair," he cried, "and they've broken it into pieces!"

"Let's get to the bottom of this," Daddy Bear growled, and they padded upstairs to the bedroom.

Daddy Bear saw the rumpled covers of his bed. "Someone's been sleeping in my bed!" he grumbled.

Mommy Bear saw the jumbled pillows on her bed. "Someone's been sleeping in *my* bed!" she said.

Baby Bear padded up to his bed. "Someone's been sleeping in my bed ...

…and they're still there!" he cried.

The three bears crowded around the sleeping girl. Baby Bear reached out a furry paw to touch her golden curls.

Goldilocks opened her eyes. Imagine her surprise when she saw three bears peering down at her!

She leaped out of the bed, ran down the stairs, through the door, along the path, and all the way home. And she never visited the house of the three bears, ever again.

The Cat That Walked
by Himself

At the very beginning of time, wild animals lived in the Wet Wild Woods. The wildest of all was Cat. He walked by himself, waving his wild tail.

One night, Dog asked Cat to go with him to the cave where Man and Woman lived. But Cat replied, "I am the cat who walks by himself, and all places are alike to me."

Dog set off for the cave, and curious Cat followed him, taking care not to be seen.

When he reached the cave, Dog said to Woman, "What is this that smells so good?"

The woman threw him a lamb bone. It was so delicious he begged for another.

"Help my Man hunt through the day and guard this cave at night," said Woman, "and I will give you as many roast bones as you need."

Later, when Man saw Dog, Woman said, "Take him with you when you go hunting. He is our friend."

Cat was listening close by. "This is a very wise woman," he thought, "but she is not as wise as I am."

A few days later, Horse asked Cat to help him search for Dog. Cat was eager to see what had happened to Dog, but because he didn't want Horse to know this, he replied, "I am the cat who walks by himself."

So Horse set off alone, not realizing that Cat was following close behind.

When Woman saw Horse, she laughed. "You did not come here for Dog, but for the sake of this hay I have." She gave him a taste, and it was wonderful.

Woman promised him lots more hay if he wore a harness on his wild head.

Later she told Man, "This servant will carry us from place to place. Ride on his back when you go hunting."

Hearing this, Cat was even more impressed with how clever Woman was.

It was Cow's turn to visit the cave next. Cow promised milk every day in return for the lush green grass around the cave. Woman agreed, and later explained to Man that the cow would provide food for them.

Listening once again, Cat decided he should talk to Woman himself.

The next day, Cat visited Woman. "I am not a friend, and I am not a servant," he told her. "I am the cat who walks by himself, and I wish to come into your cave."

The clever woman bargained with him. "I will give you warm milk three times a day forever, but only if you do three things to earn my praise."

And Cat replied, "the curtain, the fire, and the milk-pots will see that you keep your promise." Then Cat returned alone to the Wet Wild Woods.

Some time later, Cat heard there was a baby in the cave.
"Ah," he said, "my time has come."

When he reached the cave, the Woman was busy spinning and Baby was crying. Cat patted Baby with his paw, then he tickled him under his fat chin with his tail. Baby laughed and cooed.

The woman was relieved that Cat had stopped her baby from crying. "What a gentle thing!" she said.

The curtain heard Woman's praise and immediately fell to the ground.

Later, as Baby started to cry again, Cat crept close and whispered, "I will show you a magic trick." Then he tied some yarn to a piece of wood and chased it across the floor. Baby laughed as much as he had been crying.

"Clever Cat," said Woman gratefully.

The fire heard Woman praise Cat and gave a great **puff!** This was the second time she had praised Cat.

Later, when a little mouse ran across the floor, Woman jumped on the footstool, quivering, until Cat chased the mouse away.

"Thank you," she said. "You were very quick."

This was the third time Woman had praised Cat, and the milk-pot remembered her promise to provide Cat with milk. So the milk-pot cracked in two, and soon Cat was lapping up the warm milk.

That evening, Man made a further bargain with Cat.

"You can stay only if you catch mice in the cave. If you fail, I will throw you out of the cave, and so shall all men."

Dog had further conditions to add. "If you are not kind to Baby I will chase you up a tree. And so shall all dogs after me."

And so Cat kept his side of the bargain, as long as Baby didn't pull his tail too hard. He killed mice and was kind to Baby when he was in the house. But between times, and when night comes, he is the cat that walks by himself, and all places are alike to him.

The Wolf in Sheep's Clothing

There was once a wolf who lived in a forest beside a sheep farm. You might think this would mean he would never be hungry, but there was a problem. Four sheepdogs guarded the large farm, and the wolf was no match for all of them.

"I should be having lamb for dinner every night," whined the wolf. His eyes narrowed hungrily, and he drooled as he spied on the sheep from behind a bush. "Look how deliciously plump they are, feeding on that lush grass all day!"

The clever sheepdogs always made sure that one of them was awake right through the night. And if that dog so much as sniffed a wolf's scent in the air, he would bark until the farmer came running out.

"Stay away from my sheep!" the farmer would shout as the wolf fled back into the forest. "Come near my farm again and it will be the end of you!"

So as the sheep grew ever fatter, the wolf became hungrier and hungrier. He didn't know how he was going to survive.

Then one day, as he peered longingly through the trees, he noticed that the farmer was shearing the sheep. He watched as the thick woolly coats disappeared, one by one.

"I'm taking these to market," the farmer told his sheepdogs as he lifted the coats on to the back of his truck. "You keep an eye on that wolf for me."

Just as the truck was disappearing over a hill, the wolf saw one of the bundles of wool fall off the back and onto the road. A snoring sheepdog slept nearby.

The wolf suddenly had a wicked idea. Using the cover of the trees and the hedges, he sneaked along the road until he reached the bundle. He quickly unrolled it and draped the thick sheep's coat over his head and back.

"Look at me, a poor sheep who has lost his way!" he laughed.

Feeling very pleased with himself, the wolf made his way back toward the farm, being careful to keep his head near the ground.

"Baaa! Baaa!" he bleated as the four sheepdogs approached, sniffing at him.

To his delight, the sheepdogs let him pass to join their flock. The sheep also believed him, welcoming him right into their center. It was just where the wolf wanted to be, well hidden from the dogs.

"Are you hungry?" one of the sheep asked the wolf kindly.

"Yes, I am a little," the wolf bleated meekly, thinking how tasty the sheep looked. "I haven't eaten for days and days."

"Well, there's lots of lush grass here," the sheep said kindly. "You just help yourself."

The sly wolf started to plan when to pounce.

He allowed himself a little smile when one sheep told him about a wolf lurking in the forest.

"Don't worry," the sheep reassured him, "the sheepdogs won't let him get anywhere near."

His cunning plan had worked. The sheep were all fooled by his sheep's coat. All, that is, except the youngest. This small, scrawny lamb kept sniffing at the wolf. She was so new to the world that she did not know what a wolf was. But she knew what a sheep was.

"She smells different than us, Mama," the lamb bleated.

"Ah, that's probably because she's had a long, rough journey," Mother explained.

"And, look, she's got claws," the lamb said, so small that she could see right underneath the wolf's false coat. "And sharp teeth!"

At the mention of teeth, the sheep all started to bleat loudly. The deafening noise alerted the four sheepdogs, who raced toward them at once.

The wolf immediately broke free of the flock, his wool coat sliding off as he raced desperately for the trees. The dogs were right on his heels, barking fiercely.

It was only when the wolf had reached his cave right in the middle of the forest that he knew he had escaped the dogs. But his body was still trembling from head to toe.

As for the sheep, they vowed to be much more careful in the future. They would never foolishly trust a stranger again, whether he looked just like them or not.

The Little Red Hen

There was once a little red hen who lived on a farm with her friends: a sleepy cat, a lazy pig, and a very stuck-up duck.

One day, the little red hen was scratching around in the farmyard when she found some tasty grains of wheat. She was just about to peck them up when she had an idea.

"If I plant these grains instead of eating them," she said to herself, "they will grow tall and strong and make more wheat!" She tucked the grains into her apron and went to see her friends.

"Who will help me plant these grains of wheat?" she asked.

The cat opened one eye. "Not I," she said. "I'm too tired."

"Not I," snorted the pig. "It's much too hot to work."

"Not I," quacked the duck, and stood on one foot.

So the little red hen found a patch of soil. She moved the stones and dug the earth. She made a row of holes and planted all the grains of wheat. Then she watered them carefully and left them to grow.

All summer, the sun shone on the grains of wheat and the rain fell on them. Each day, the little red hen checked that they were not too dry or too wet. She pulled up the weeds and made sure the wheat had space to grow. At last, the wheat was strong and tall with fat, golden grains.

"This wheat is ready to harvest," she said to herself. "That will be a lot of work." The little red hen went to see her friends.

"I have worked all summer and the wheat is ready. Who will help me harvest it?" she asked.

The cat stretched lazily. "Not I," she said. "It's time for my afternoon nap."

"Not I," snorted the pig. "I need to roll in the mud."

"Not I," quacked the duck, and she preened her feathers.

So the little red hen took her tools and went to harvest the wheat. She cut down the wheat stalks and piled them up neatly. When she had finished, she went back to her friends.

"I have worked all day to cut down the wheat," she said. "Who will help me prepare the wheat for the mill?"

The cat yawned. "Not I," she said. "I'm still sleepy."

"Not I," snorted the pig. "I'm going to lie in the sun."

"Not I," quacked the duck, and tucked her head under her wing.

So the little red hen went back to the field alone. She beat the wheat to free the grains from the stalks, and carried away the straw. The wind blew, and the little red hen worked long and hard. At last, she swept up the wheat and put it into a sack. She carried it back to her friends.

"I have worked all day to prepare the wheat," she said. "Who will help me carry it to the mill?"

"Not I," said the cat. "I need to rest."

"Not I," snorted the pig. "It looks much too heavy."

"Not I," quacked the duck, and she waddled away to the pond.

So the little red hen carried the heavy sack of wheat all the way to the mill. The kind miller ground the wheat to flour and poured it back into the sack. Then the little red hen carried it all the way home again.

The little red hen was exhausted.

"I have carried the wheat to the mill and had it ground to flour," she said. "Who will help me bake it into bread?"

"Not I," said the cat, and she curled up, ready to sleep.

"Not I," snorted the pig. "It's nearly time for my dinner."

"Not I," quacked the duck, and she sat on the ground.

So the little red hen made the flour into dough and kneaded it. She shaped it into a loaf and put it in the oven to bake. After a while, a delicious smell wafted from the kitchen. The sleepy cat opened her eyes. The lazy pig came to stand by the oven. The stuck-up duck waddled in.

At last, the bread was baked. The little red hen carried the loaf to the table. It had a beautiful golden crust on the top and was creamy white inside. It smelled wonderful.

"Who will help me eat this loaf of bread?" the little red hen asked quietly.

"I will!" said the sleepy cat, washing her paws.

"I will!" grunted the lazy pig, licking his lips.

"I will!" quacked the stuck-up duck, flapping her wings.

"No, you will not!" the little red hen said. "I planted the grains and watched them grow. I harvested the wheat and took it to the mill. I ground the flour and baked the bread. My chicks and I will eat the loaf!"

And that is what they did. The little red hen and her tiny chicks ate up every crumb of the hot, fresh bread.

Wild Swans

Far away, in a magical land, there lived a king who had eleven sons and one precious daughter, Elise.

When their father remarried, the children's lives changed forever. The evil stepmother was cruel to them, and very soon she sent Elise away to be brought up by peasants.

Then she cast a spell on the boys.

"Fly away in the form of great speechless birds," she cried. And, at that, the sons changed into white swans with huge flapping wings. They flew out of the windows and far away from the palace.

After many years, the king defied his wife and sent for his daughter to live at the palace again.

The queen was jealous of the young girl's beauty, so before Elise was presented to her father she had her golden hair tangled and face dirtied with walnut juice.

"You are not my daughter!" cried the king when he saw her.

Elise ran far away into the forest. Lost and tired, she lay down to rest. All night she dreamed of her brothers, who she missed dearly. She knew her stepmother had done something wicked to them.

When she awoke, Elise bathed in a fresh pool in the forest, washing away the evil work of the queen.

Elise came across an old woman carrying a basket of berries, and asked hopefully, "Have you seen eleven princes?"

"No," the woman replied. "But yesterday I saw eleven swans with crowns on their heads swimming down at the brook."

"My brothers!" Elise cried.

The old woman led Elise to the stream. There, Elise waited. At last, at sunset, she spotted eleven wild swans with golden crowns flying toward the land. When the sun disappeared, so did the swans. They transformed into the eleven princes. Elise let out a cry of joy as she ran to hug her brothers.

"Every morning at sunrise, we turn into swans," the eldest brother explained. "We spend the day flying and then return to our human form at sunset."

"Please come with us tomorrow, Elise," begged the youngest brother. Elise gladly agreed.

The brothers wove a mat out of willow bark to carry their sister. When morning came, they turned back into swans, and taking the mat in their beaks, they carried Elise through the sky. All day long, they flew across the ocean.

65

Finally, as night fell, they settled down to sleep. As she slept, Elise had a dream that a fairy told her:

"Your brothers can be freed, but only if you weave eleven shirts out of stinging nettles. Until you have completed the task, you must not say a word, or else their lives will be in danger."

When Elise woke, she spent all her time weaving the shirts. The nettles stung her terribly, and before long her hands were covered with blisters, but Elise persevered.

One day as she was sewing, she looked up to find a handsome king standing before her. When he asked her name, she was unable to speak.

Struck by her beauty, and concerned for her safety, the king reached out his hand. "Come with me," he said.

The king took her to his palace, where she was lavished with riches. But Elise could only mourn silently for her brothers, and the king did not understand what she was trying to tell him.

Some people in the court were suspicious of Elise, but this did not bother the king, and he married her.

But when Elise was spotted picking nettles from the churchyard, whispers began that she was a witch who wanted to destroy the kingdom.

One night as Elise creeped out of the chamber, the king followed her to the eerie churchyard where he watched her pick some nettles.

"It is true. She is a witch!" he cried.

The king reluctantly banished Elise from the palace, and the court plotted revenge.

Elise did not despair as she slept among the nettles, because she knew that she could now finish the shirts for her brothers.

Just as Elise began work on the final sleeve of the very last shirt, she was captured by angry townspeople.

She was loaded into a cart and brought to market square, where an angry crowd was waiting next to a burning fire.

Suddenly, eleven wild swans surrounded her, flapping their wings in desperation. Elise had carried with her the eleven shirts and quickly threw them over the swans.

One by one they turned back into princes, but as Elise had not quite finished the last shirt, her youngest brother still had one snow-white wing.

The curse was lifted.

"Now I can speak! I am not a witch!" she cried.

Her brothers surrounded her and called out, "She is innocent."

The crowd could hardly believe what they had just witnessed. They now knew this girl was not a witch.

"Forgive me," the king begged.

"Of course," Elise replied.

As the church bells rang out, and the crowd cheered, the king declared he would give each of Elise's brothers a portion of the kingdom.

They ruled wisely and with great kindness, always grateful to their devoted sister.

The Lion and the Mouse

Once upon a time, there was a lion who lived in a dark, rocky den in the middle of the jungle. When the lion wasn't out hunting, he loved to curl up in his den and sleep. In fact, as his friends knew, if he didn't get enough sleep, the lion became extremely grumpy.

One day, while the lion lay snoozing in his cave, a little mouse came scurrying past. The mouse lived with his family beneath a tall tree on the other side of the lion's rocky home.

He was on his way back for supper and didn't want to have to climb up and over the big boulders, so he thought he'd take a short cut straight through the lion's den.

"What harm can it do?" he thought. "He's snoring so loudly, he'll never hear me."

But as he passed the snoring beast ... he accidentally ran over the lion's paw!

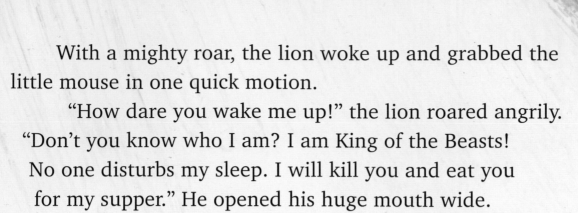

With a mighty roar, the lion woke up and grabbed the little mouse in one quick motion.

"How dare you wake me up!" the lion roared angrily. "Don't you know who I am? I am King of the Beasts! No one disturbs my sleep. I will kill you and eat you for my supper." He opened his huge mouth wide.

Shaking with fear at the sight of all the lion's sharp, pointed teeth, the terrified little mouse begged the angry lion to let him go.

"Please, Your Majesty," he cried. "I didn't mean to wake you up. It was an accident. I was just trying to get home to my family. I'm too small to make a good meal for someone as mighty as you. Let me go and I promise to help you one day."

The grumpy lion stared at the little mouse. Then he laughed loudly. "You help me?" he said scornfully, shaking his furry mane. "Ha! Ha! Ha! What a ridiculous idea! You're too small to help someone as big as me."

The little mouse trembled and closed his eyes as he waited for the terrible jaws to snap him up.

But to his surprise, the lion didn't eat him. Instead, he smiled and opened his paw.

"Go home, little mouse," said the lion. "You have made me laugh and put me in a good mood, so I will let you live. But hurry, before I change my mind."

The little mouse was very grateful. "Thank you, Your Majesty!" he squeaked. "I promise to be your friend forever, and I won't disturb you again."

As quickly as he could, the little mouse scurried home. What a story he would have to tell his children!

A few days later, the lion was out hunting in the jungle. As he creeped stealthily through the lush undergrowth, he smelled something delicious. There, in a small clearing just ahead of him, stood a goat, eating the grass beneath a shady tree.

The lion circled the clearing, slowly crawling through the tall grass. He crouched low, ready to pounce on the unsuspecting goat … when suddenly a big net fell on him.

He was trapped in a hunter's snare!

The goat, bleating in terror, ran off into the jungle. The lion roared and tried to break free from the trap. But the more he struggled, the more he became tangled in the net. He was so angry that he let out the loudest of roars.

The trees in the jungle shook with the terrible noise. Every animal for miles heard it, including the little mouse.

"Oh no!" squeaked the mouse. "That's my friend, the lion. He must be in trouble! I've got to go and help him."

"Be careful, my dear," cried the mouse's wife. "Remember how big he is!"

The little mouse scurried through the jungle as fast as his tiny legs would carry him, toward the lion's mighty roar.

Soon he came upon the clearing and the lion, tangled and trapped in the ropes of the hunter's net.

"Keep still, Your Majesty," cried the mouse. "I'll have you out of there in no time."

"You?" laughed the lion.

The mouse ignored him and quickly started gnawing through the net with his sharp little teeth.

Before long, there was a big hole in the net, and the lion squeezed through the ropes and escaped his trap.

The lion held out his giant paw toward the little mouse. "Thank you, my little friend," he said humbly, bowing his huge head.

"I was wrong when I laughed at you and said that someone as small as you couldn't help me. You saved my life today, and I am truly grateful."

The little mouse smiled up at the lion. "You were kind enough to let me go before, and I promised I would pay you back one day," he squeaked. "It was my turn to help you."

Side by side, the big lion and little mouse walked back into the jungle. From that day on the huge, mighty lion and the tiny, mighty mouse were the best of friends.

The Frog Prince

Once upon a time, there was a king whose castle lay in the heart of a great forest. All his daughters were beautiful, but the youngest princess was the most radiant of them all. Everyone in the royal court loved her. Servants followed her everywhere, desperate to please her. Ladies-in-waiting helped her get dressed, butlers served her breakfast, and musicians played to her as she wandered through the castle gardens. Crowds trailed after the princess night and day, desperate to earn one of her lovely smiles.

Whenever the princess needed some time alone, she would make an excuse to slip away from court. She knew a winding path that led into the shadiest part of the forest. At the end of the trail there was a little nook with a well in the middle. The princess liked to lean over and dabble her fingers in the clear water. The well was small but deep, bubbling gently in the dappled light. The princess's happiest times were spent there.

"This is my favorite place in the whole kingdom," she would murmur. "I hope I will always be able to spend time here."

The princess spent many happy days sitting beside the well. She often thought of her mother as she listened to the water and felt the wind on her cheeks. Her mother had died when the princess was a very small child, but when she was alone at the well the princess felt her mother's love more strongly than ever.

One day at the well, the princess brought a toy her mother had given her. It was a little ball made of pure gold.

The princess started to throw it higher and higher, clapping her hands before reaching out to catch it. She threw it once more, laughing as the ball glimmered in the sunlight. But this time it slipped through her fingers and disappeared into the well.

"Oh no!" cried the princess, peering over the edge. "Mother's gift!"

The princess gazed deep into the water for a glint of gold, but the ball had vanished.

"My beautiful ball is gone forever," the princess said sadly.

She sank down on the grass and wept with her face in her hands. After a few minutes, she heard a raspy voice.

"Princess, why are you crying?" said the voice. It was coming from the well.

The princess leaned over the side of the well and saw something rippling the surface of the water. Then a warty green frog lifted its head out of the water and gazed up at her through bulging eyes.

"Please tell me," he said. "What is the matter?"

"I dropped my golden ball into the water," she explained. "I am sad because it has gone forever."

The frog scrambled up onto the side of the well. "I can bring your ball back up for you," he said. "But what will you do for me?"

The princess's face suddenly shone with hope. The frog was slimy and revolting, but she didn't care. At that moment, he was her only chance.

"Dear frog," she said, "I will give anything you want."

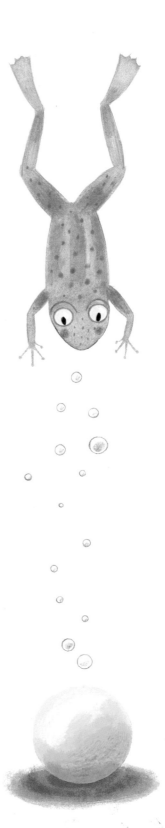

"I am lonely, and I just want to be your friend," he said.

The princess nodded eagerly. "Of course," she replied.

"I want to eat from your plate when I'm hungry," he went on, "drink from your cup when I'm thirsty, and sleep on your pillow when I am tired. Promise me that I will be a true friend."

The princess hesitated. "I promise," she said.

Satisfied, the frog leaped back into the well. A few moments later, the princess saw the golden shimmer of her ball rising up through the water.

The princess gave a cry of delight and hugged the ball to her chest. Then she turned and ran off toward the castle.

"Wait for me!" the frog croaked. "I am too small to keep up!"

The princess ran all the way back to the castle, dashed up to her bedroom, and slammed the door behind her.

By the next day, the princess had quite forgotten about the ugly little frog with the bulging eyes.

That evening at supper, the great dining hall was quiet as the royal family began to eat.

Drip-drop! Drip-drop!

"What's that noise?" asked the king. "It's coming from the door."

Drip-drop! Drip-drop!

He clicked his fingers, and a footman hurried to open it.

The youngest princess dropped her fork, and it clattered onto her plate.

The frog was sitting in the doorway. "Dear princess, I've come to be with you," he rasped. "A true friendship, in return for your golden ball. Just as you promised."

The princess shuddered and looked at her father.

"Send him away, please Father?" she asked with her most charming smile.

To her surprise, he frowned. "A promise always counts, whether it is made to a frog or a king," he said. "You must invite him in."

The frog slurped and squelched his way through dinner, and to the princess's disgust he insisted on eating from her plate.

"I am full," he said at last. "Please carry me upstairs, dear friend, so that I can sleep beside you on your pillow."

Hot tears pricked the princess's eyes as she picked him up and took him to her bed chamber.

When the princess imagined the frog crouching on her white sheets, smearing them with gravy and slime and muddy water, she could bear it no longer.

She threw him across the room with all her strength. He dropped to the floor and lay there, still and silent. "No!" she cried out, regretting her actions instantly. "What have I done? I didn't mean to hurt you." At that moment the frog didn't seem ugly or disgusting. He just looked weak and sad.

The princess scooped him up in her gentle hands and drew him close to her, placing a light kiss upon his head.

"I am sorry from the bottom of my heart," she whispered. "Please forgive me, poor lonely frog."

"I will gladly accept your apology," replied a deep, rich voice.

Where the frog had once been there was now a handsome young man, smiling at her.

"But where—what—wh—who are you?" the princess asked.

"I am a prince," replied the man. "A witch cursed me many years ago. She turned me into a frog and threw me down the well."

"That's awful," said the princess. "How did you break the spell?"

"I didn't," said the prince. "You broke it for me with a kiss of true, loving friendship."

The princess's cheeks flushed.

"I wasn't a true or loving friend at first," she said. "I didn't think that I could ever care about a frog. I was wrong."

"It was our destiny to meet this way," said the prince, dropping to one knee. "Dear princess, will you promise to be my wife one day?"

The princess kneeled beside him and put her arms around him.

"I will," she said. "It was a lucky day when I dropped my ball in the well, and I will never break a promise again."

Puss in Boots

There was once an old miller who had three sons whom he loved dearly. When the miller died, he left the mill to his oldest son. The middle son was given the donkeys. The youngest son, a kind man who had always put his father and brothers before himself, was left nothing but his father's cat.

"What will become of me?" said the miller's young son with a sigh, looking at his cat.

"Buy me a fine pair of boots and I will help you make your fortune, for your father thought you deserved it," replied the cat.

A talking cat! The miller's son could not believe his ears. Nevertheless, he bought the cat a fine pair of boots, and the two of them set off to seek their fortune. After a while, they came to a grand palace.

"Wouldn't it be wonderful to live so grandly," sighed the miller's son.

Later, while the miller's son was sleeping, the cat went hunting and caught a rabbit. He put it in a sack and took it to the palace.

"A gift to the king from my esteemed master, the Marquis of Carabas," said the cat, presenting the rabbit.

The cat went back to the miller's son and told him what he had done.

"Now the king will want to know who the Marquis of Carabas is," laughed the cat.

A clever cat! The miller's son could not believe his ears.

Every day for a week, the cat delivered a gift to the king, each time saying it was from the Marquis of Carabas.

After a while, the king became very curious and decided he'd like his daughter to meet this mysterious nobleman, whoever he might be.

When the cat heard that the king and his daughter were on their way, he wasted no time.

"You must take off all your clothes and stand in the river," the cat told his master.

The puzzled miller's son did as he was told, and the cat hid his master's tattered old clothes behind a rock.

When the cat heard the king's carriage approaching, he jumped onto the road and begged for help.

"Your gracious majesty," said the cat, "my master was robbed of all his clothes while he was bathing in the river."

The king gave the miller's son a suit of fine clothes to wear.

"Please join us in the carriage," said the king.

So the cat opened the door and the miller's son climbed in. He looked very handsome in his new suit. The king's daughter fell in love with him at once.

The cat ran on, cutting through the surrounding countryside. Every time he met people working in the fields, he told them, "If the king stops to ask who owns this land, you must tell him it belongs to the Marquis of Carabas."

Beyond the fields, the cat reached a grand castle. He spoke to the people working in a field next to it and discovered that it belonged to a fierce ogre.

The cat stood bravely in his boots and knocked on the castle door.

"Who dares to disturb me?" roared a voice from inside the castle walls.

"I have heard that you are a very clever ogre," called the cat. "I have come to see what tricks you can do."

The ogre opened the door and immediately changed himself into a great snarling lion. The cat felt scared, but he didn't show it.

"That is quite a clever trick," said the cat, "but a lion is a very large creature. I think it would be a much better trick to change into something very small, like a mouse."

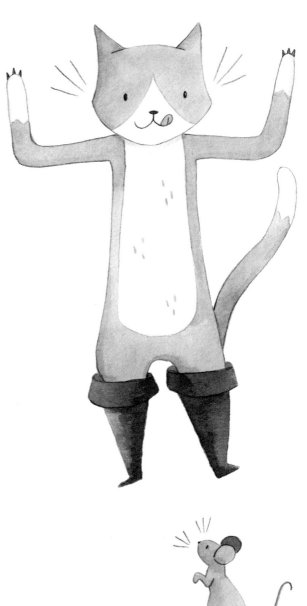

The ogre liked to show off his magic tricks. He changed at once into a little mouse, but as soon as he did so the cat pounced on the mouse and ate him up!

Then the cat went into the castle and told all of the servants that their new master was the Marquis of Carabas. They were glad to be rid of the fierce ogre, so they did not complain.

"The king is on his way to visit, and you must prepare a grand feast to welcome him," said the cat.

When the king's carriage arrived at the castle, the cat was waiting to welcome him.

"Your gracious majesty," he purred, "welcome to the home of my master, the Marquis of Carabas."

A cunning cat! The miller's son could not believe his eyes.

"You must ask for the princess's hand in marriage," the cunning cat whispered to his master.

The miller's son did as he was told.

The king, who was impressed by everything he saw, agreed.

Soon, the Marquis of Carabas and his wife were married, and they lived a very happy life together. The cat was made a lord of their court and was given the most splendid clothes, which he wore proudly along with those fine boots that the miller's son had bought him.

The Nightingale

The Emperor of China once lived in a palace so magnificent that travelers would come from all over the world just to admire it. They returned home and wrote books about the delicate porcelain palace and its beautiful garden where little silver bells were tied to the prettiest flowers and tinkled as you passed by. But most of all, they wrote about the Nightingale, with his exquisite voice that brought joy to all who heard him sing.

"How can there be such a bird in my empire, in my own garden, that I've never seen?" the Emperor exclaimed when he read their accounts. And he demanded that the Nightingale should be brought to the palace to sing for him.

The palace officials searched high and low for the Nightingale, but without success. At last they found a kitchen girl who told them, "I know him well. Every evening I hear the Nightingale sing. It brings tears to my eyes." And she took them into the forest, where the tiny bird willingly burst into song.

The Lord-in-Waiting was mightily impressed and invited the Nightingale to the palace. "My song is best heard in the woods," the little bird told him humbly. But when he heard it was the Emperor's wish for him to sing at the palace, the Nightingale went willingly.

There was huge excitement in the palace. The flowers with tinkling bells were brought inside the grand hall, and in the middle of the throne room where the Emperor sat, a special golden cage was arranged for the Nightingale.

When his moment came, the little bird sang so sweetly that he melted the Emperor's heart. The Emperor offered to reward him with a golden slipper, but the little bird declined.

"I have seen tears in the Emperor's eyes," he said, "I have my reward."

So he was invited to stay at court and was given his own cage. Twelve footmen took him out to fly twice a day and once at night. Each one held a ribbon tied to the Nightingale's leg. The little bird was soon the talk of the land.

One day the Emperor received an artificial nightingale encrusted with diamonds, rubies, and sapphires. When it was wound up, it sang one of the Nightingale's songs, over and over again. The courtiers soon began to prefer this bird as it sang as well as the Nightingale but looked prettier with all its sparkling jewels. So the real Nightingale flew back to his home in the forest.

The artificial bird had its own cushion beside the Emperor's bed and was given the title "Grand Imperial Singer-of-the-Emperor-to-Sleep." After a year, every person in China knew the song of the artificial bird, and wherever you went, you could hear children singing, **"Zizizi! Kluk, kluk, kluk."**

But then one night, something inside the bird broke. Its song was silenced forever.

Five years passed, and sorrow engulfed the whole country. China's much-loved Emperor fell ill, and the country prepared for a new leader.

"Sing!" the sick Emperor called weakly to the artificial bird. "Sing, my little bird! I have given you gold and precious presents. Sing, I pray you, sing!"

But the bird stood silent.

Suddenly, through the window came a burst of song. It was the real Nightingale. And as he sang, the blood flowed quicker and quicker through the Emperor's feeble body.

"Thank you, thank you!" the Emperor cried. "Little bird from Heaven, you have sung away the sadness. How can I ever repay you?"

"You have already rewarded me," said the Nightingale. "I brought tears to your eyes when first I sang for you. Sleep now, and grow fresh and strong while I sing."

"You must stay with me always," said the Emperor. "I shall break the artificial bird into a thousand pieces."

"No," said the Nightingale. "It did its best. Keep it near you. I cannot live in a palace, so let me come as I will. Then I shall sit by your window and sing things that will make you happy. A little singing bird flies far and wide, to the fisherman's hut, to the farmer's home, and to many other places a long way off. I will come and sing to you, if you will promise me one thing."

"All that I have is yours," said the Emperor, smiling.

"You must not let anyone know that you have a little bird who tells you everything." And away he flew.

Early the next day, when the servants came expecting to find their Emperor very sick, they were astonished to hear him speak.

"I am quite recovered," he said, standing proudly in his fine robes. "And I think I'll rule for some years yet."

The Three Billy Goats Gruff

Once upon a time, there were three goats — a little white one, a medium-sized brown one, and a big gray one. They were the Billy Goats Gruff and they were brothers.

The little Billy Goat Gruff had little horns.

The medium-sized Billy Goat Gruff had medium-sized horns.

And the big Billy Goat Gruff had big, curly horns!

The three brothers lived in a small meadow beside a river. All day long they ate the green grass.

On the other side of the river, over a rickety wooden bridge, was a huge field. The Billy Goats thought the grass there looked longer and greener and juicier!

Day after day, the three Billy Goats Gruff looked longingly at the juicy grass on the other side of the river. They would have happily crossed the bridge to go there, except for one thing.

One horrible thing. A mean and smelly old troll with very pointy teeth lived under the bridge, and he guarded it day and night.

The grass in the meadow where the three Billy Goats Gruff lived got shorter and shorter, and drier and browner, and the brothers were getting hungrier and hungrier for fresh, juicy grass.

One day, the little Billy Goat Gruff decided he'd had enough. "I'm so hungry!" he cried to his brothers. "I can't eat one more blade of this dry, brown grass."

"We agree!" groaned his two brothers. "Look at that juicy grass over there. Oh, if only we could get past the mean old troll."

"I'm going to try," said the little Billy Goat Gruff bravely. And off he set, **TRIP TRAP, TRIP TRAP,** across the bridge.

Suddenly a croaky voice roared out, "Who's that **TRIP TRAPPING** over my bridge? I'll eat you if you pass. You'd taste yummy in a sandwich!"

"Oh, please don't eat me," cried the little goat. He was very frightened, but he had a plan. "I'm only a little goat. My brother will be crossing in a minute, and he is much bigger and tastier than me!"

The greedy troll thought about this and burped loudly. "All right," he said, "you may cross."

The little Billy Goat Gruff ran as fast as his little legs would take him until he reached the other side.

The medium-sized goat saw his little brother munching the juicy grass on the other side of the river. He really wanted to eat that grass, too.

He turned to the big Billy Goat Gruff. "If he can cross the bridge, then so can I!" he said. And off he set, **TRIP TRAP, TRIP TRAP**, across the bridge.

Suddenly, the mean troll climbed out from his hiding place. "Who's that **TRIP TRAPPING** over my bridge? I'll eat you if you pass. You'd taste nice with rice!" He licked his lips when he noticed how much bigger this goat was.

The medium-sized Billy Goat Gruff stopped, his hooves clacking together in fear. "Oh, please don't eat me," he cried. "I'm really not that big. My brother will be crossing in a minute, and he is so much bigger and tastier than me!"

The troll rolled his eyes, licked dribble from his chin, and grunted that the medium-sized goat could cross the bridge.

The medium-sized Billy Goat Gruff galloped quickly across the bridge to join his little brother, before the mean troll changed his mind.

The big Billy Goat Gruff had been watching his brothers.

"I'm big and strong … and I'm really hungry!" he said to himself. So off he set, **TRIP TRAP, TRIP TRAP,** across the bridge to join his brothers and eat the juicy green grass on the other side.

As before, the mean, smelly troll scrabbled up onto the bridge. "Who's that **TRIP TRAPPING** over my bridge? I'll eat you if you pass. You'd taste scrumptious in a stew!" This goat was big! The troll's mouth started watering and his large tummy started rumbling.

The big Billy Goat Gruff stamped his hooves. "No, you can't eat me!" he shouted. "I'm big and I have big horns, and I will toss you into the river if you don't let me pass."

Before the troll could answer, the big Billy Goat Gruff put his head down and charged at him. He tossed the mean creature high up into the air.

DOWN, DOWN, DOWN

fell the troll.

With a huge splash, he dropped into the river and floated away. And that was the end of the mean troll.

"Well done, big brother!" laughed the little Billy Goat Gruff and the medium-sized Billy Goat Gruff. "Come and eat this grass—it is truly juicy and delicious!"

And the three Billy Goats Gruff were never hungry again.

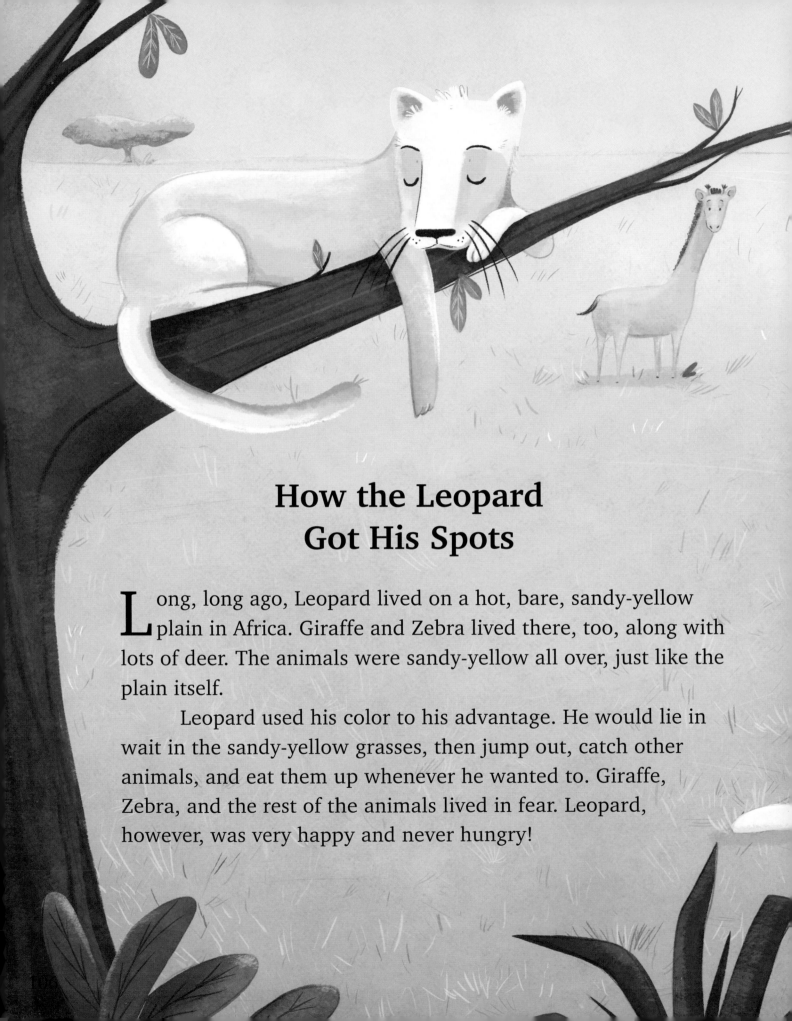

How the Leopard
Got His Spots

Long, long ago, Leopard lived on a hot, bare, sandy-yellow plain in Africa. Giraffe and Zebra lived there, too, along with lots of deer. The animals were sandy-yellow all over, just like the plain itself.

Leopard used his color to his advantage. He would lie in wait in the sandy-yellow grasses, then jump out, catch other animals, and eat them up whenever he wanted to. Giraffe, Zebra, and the rest of the animals lived in fear. Leopard, however, was very happy and never hungry!

After a while, the other animals were fed up. They decided to move away from the sandy plain to find a better place to live. They walked and walked until they came to a huge forest where the sun shone through the trees making stripy, speckly, patchy shadows, and sections of spotty, stripy sunshine.

The animals hid themselves there, and while they hid, partly in the sun, partly in the shadows, their skins changed color.

Giraffe's skin became covered with big, brown, blotchy spots from the blotchy shadow he stood in, and Zebra's skin became covered with stripes from the stripy shadow he lay in. The other animals' skin became darker, too, with wavy lines and patterns from the shadows around them.

Back on the sandy plain, Leopard was puzzled. All of his prey had disappeared, and he was starting to get hungry.

"Where have they all gone?" he asked Baboon.

"To the forest," said Baboon carelessly. "And they've changed. You need to change, too."

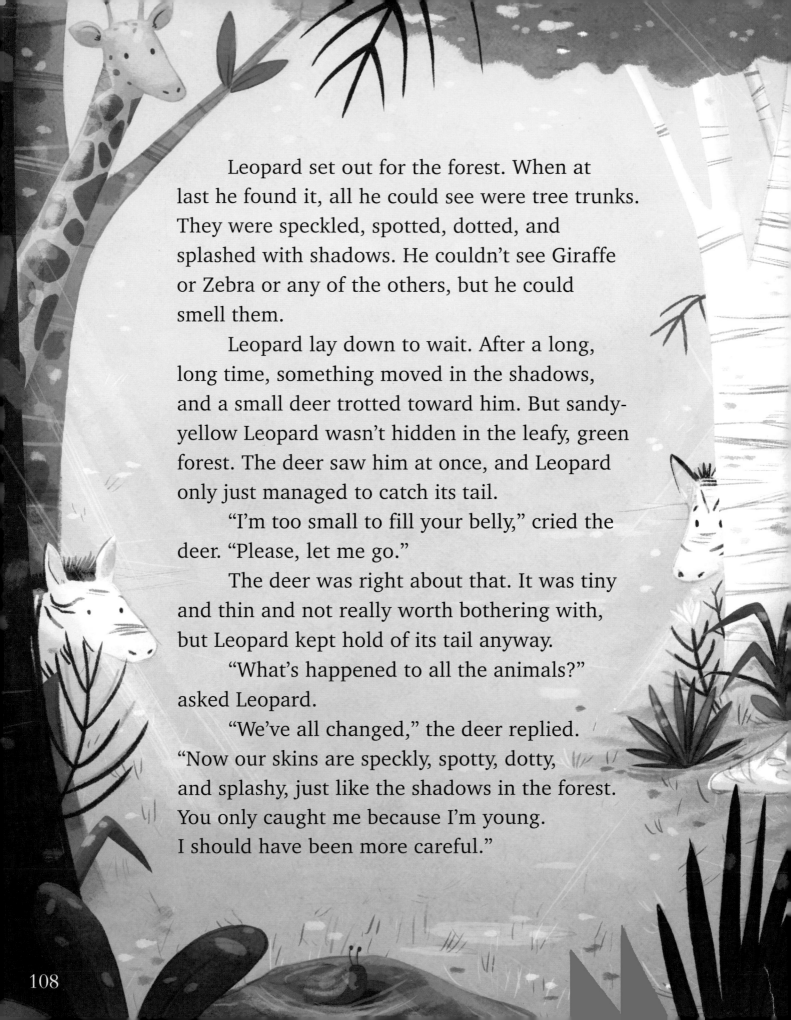

Leopard set out for the forest. When at last he found it, all he could see were tree trunks. They were speckled, spotted, dotted, and splashed with shadows. He couldn't see Giraffe or Zebra or any of the others, but he could smell them.

Leopard lay down to wait. After a long, long time, something moved in the shadows, and a small deer trotted toward him. But sandy-yellow Leopard wasn't hidden in the leafy, green forest. The deer saw him at once, and Leopard only just managed to catch its tail.

"I'm too small to fill your belly," cried the deer. "Please, let me go."

The deer was right about that. It was tiny and thin and not really worth bothering with, but Leopard kept hold of its tail anyway.

"What's happened to all the animals?" asked Leopard.

"We've all changed," the deer replied. "Now our skins are speckly, spotty, dotty, and splashy, just like the shadows in the forest. You only caught me because I'm young. I should have been more careful."

Leopard let the little deer go and sat down to think. "So that's why I can't see Giraffe and Zebra and the rest of them in the forest," he thought. "How am I ever going to catch them again if they can see me coming?"

As he sat there thinking, more deer walked through the trees. When they moved, Leopard could see them clearly. When they stopped moving, they were hidden by the shadows.

Leopard sat in the shadows a long, long time and licked his paws thoughtfully. Soon, he began to notice something odd. His paws weren't sandy-yellow any more. They had small, dark spots on them. There were spots on his tail, too.

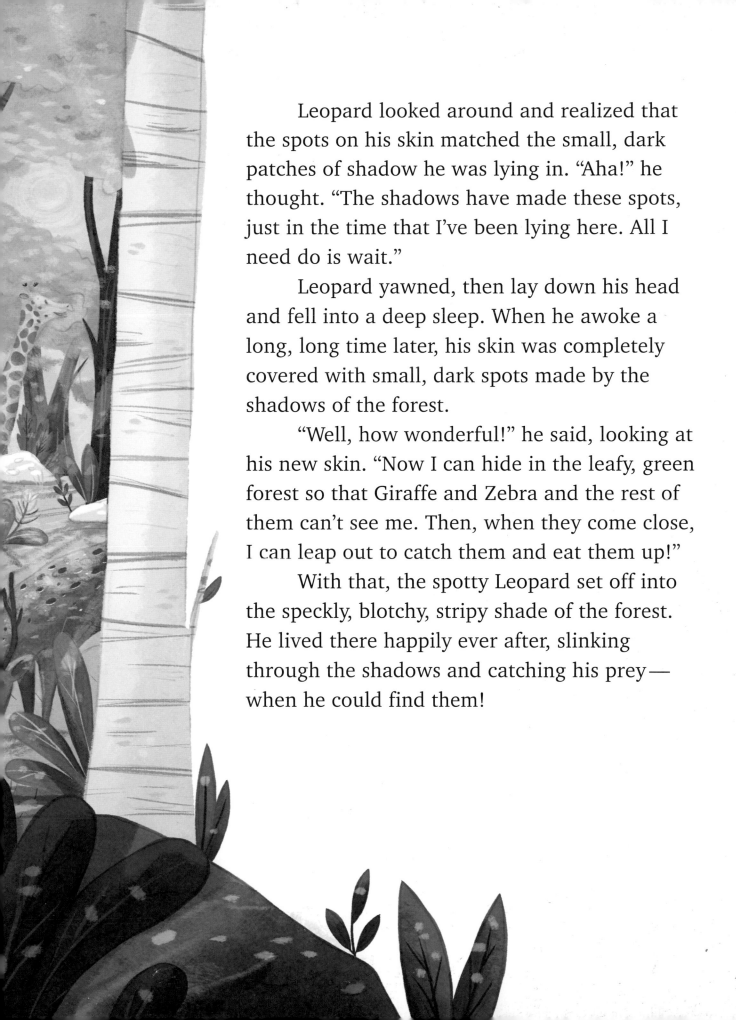

Leopard looked around and realized that the spots on his skin matched the small, dark patches of shadow he was lying in. "Aha!" he thought. "The shadows have made these spots, just in the time that I've been lying here. All I need do is wait."

Leopard yawned, then lay down his head and fell into a deep sleep. When he awoke a long, long time later, his skin was completely covered with small, dark spots made by the shadows of the forest.

"Well, how wonderful!" he said, looking at his new skin. "Now I can hide in the leafy, green forest so that Giraffe and Zebra and the rest of them can't see me. Then, when they come close, I can leap out to catch them and eat them up!"

With that, the spotty Leopard set off into the speckly, blotchy, stripy shade of the forest. He lived there happily ever after, slinking through the shadows and catching his prey— when he could find them!

The Peacock and the Crane

Every day, Peacock liked to parade up and down the riverbank near his home, showing off his splendid shimmering tail feathers to anyone who happened to be passing by. He flounced and strutted, admiring his reflection in the river.

"Look at me!" he would cry. "I'm so handsome, no other creature can compare to me."

One fine morning, Peacock was taking his usual stroll along the riverbank. A crane, who was catching fish in the shallow waters at the edge of the river, stopped to watch him. The sunlight glinted off the dazzling blues and greens and yellows of Peacock's long tail feathers, which swept the ground behind Peacock in a majestic trail.

Crane's own feathers were dull and plain, so she stared in wonder at the beautiful sight.

"Oh, wouldn't it be lovely to have such splendid and colorful feathers," she sighed.

Peacock turned to admire his reflection and saw Crane staring at him. He fanned out his tail haughtily.

"I'm not surprised you are admiring me," he said, looking down his beak. "What dreary feathers you have!"

Poor Crane didn't know what to say. She bowed her long neck down to the water to hide her shame.

"Just look at your funny neck and knobbly knees," crowed Peacock nastily. He pulled glimmering tail feathers around him. "I'd be embarrassed!"

Crane looked up at the intricate patterns of Peacock's feathers. It was like hundreds of sparkling rainbow-colored eyes were looking back at her, staring at her own plain, ugly feathers.

"You'll never be as beautiful as me," said Peacock. With a satisfied swish of his gorgeous tail, he continued his stroll.

"It's true," thought Crane sadly to herself. "Look at everyone admiring Peacock. No one looks at me like that."

Flapping her strong wings, Crane rose into the air and flew off to perch in a nearby tree. Deep in her heart, she knew she shouldn't feel envious. After all, Peacock was rude and mean, and not many of the other animals really liked him. Yet, she couldn't help looking at him.

All that day, and for several days afterward, Crane watched Peacock as he moved around. She was careful to stay out of his way, but she couldn't help overhearing his boastful comments or noticing the rude way in which he treated everyone.

"You could use my feathers to make a gorgeous gown fit for a queen," Peacock said to a flock of sparrows one day. "Your feathers are no good for anything other than stuffing pillows."

"Your feathers are so dull and plain," Peacock said to a crow another time. "You should make more of an effort to be like me. Why don't you decorate them with some of my old ones so that you don't look so awful?"

Crane noticed that at the end of each day, as the sun dipped behind the horizon, Peacock made his way to the same tree. There, with a big show of flapping his wings and an awkward jump, he flew clumsily up to a low branch to roost for the night.

Crane was curious, so one evening, she decided to visit Peacock. "Every night, you roost on the lowest branch in this tree," she said. "Why don't you fly up higher? You'd be much safer, especially since the fox has been prowling around here the last few days."

With a haughty turn of his head, Peacock snapped, "I can't fly any higher. My splendid tail is too long and heavy."

Crane was surprised. "Oh dear," she said. "What a shame. You mean to say that you've never soared through the sky on a beautiful sunny day? It is such a wonderful feeling!"

"Why would I ever want to do that?" snapped Peacock.

"And you've never flown through a velvet night with the light of the moon and the stars shining down on you?" continued Crane. "It's amazing!"

"No!" shouted Peacock. "Why would I waste time doing that? If I want to see something amazing, I only have to look at my own beautiful feathers or gaze at my glorious reflection."

Crane couldn't believe how vain and arrogant Peacock was. Suddenly, she smiled to herself.

Crane had been comparing herself to Peacock all week, but now she realized that she didn't need to.

"Dear Peacock, it is true that you have beautiful feathers," she said, "and that my black-and-white feathers are plain. But at least I can use my dull feathers to fly with and soar through the sky!"

"How dare you speak to me like that!" cried Peacock. "You are just jealous of me."

Crane spread her broad wings and flapped them gently. "I certainly don't envy you anymore," she said. "I can soar freely, while you are forever stuck on the ground!"

With that, Crane flew up into the night sky and away under the splendid, silvery light of the moon.

The Wolf and the Seven Little Kids

A wise Mother Goat and her seven little kids lived in a pretty cottage on the edge of a forest. One day, Mother Goat needed to go to the market.

"You are now all old enough to be left at home alone," she said to her children. "But watch out for the Big Bad Wolf. He will try to trick you into letting him in. Unless you hear my high, sweet voice and see my soft, white feet do not open the door."

Not long after their mother left for the market, there was a **knock, knock, knock** on the door.

"Who's there?" asked the oldest kid.

"It's your mother. Let me in!" said a deep, rough voice.

"Our mother's voice is sweet and high," said the youngest kid. "You're the wolf. Go away!"

The wolf knew he needed to find a way to trick the goats, so he went and bought some honey.

"This will make my voice so sweet that the little kids will think I'm their mother," he said to himself. He drank the honey, ran back to the goat's house and knocked on the door once more.

"Let me in, children! It's your mother, back from the market," called the wolf.

"This voice is high and sweet just like Mother's," said the oldest goat. "I'll open the door."

But just as he was about to turn the handle, the youngest goat spotted the wolf's hairy, gray feet.

"It's a trick!" she said. "Our mother's feet are white. You're the wolf. Go away!"

The wolf needed another plan, so he went to the baker and bought some flour. He rubbed it all over his legs until his feet looked white.

Then he ran back to the goat's house and knocked on the door a third time.

"Children, I'm home," he said in his high, sweet voice. "Let me in!"

"Show us your feet first," said the oldest kid. The wolf put one of his soft, white feet up to the window.

"It is Mother!" said the kids. They opened the door, and the clever wolf came running in.

"Hide!" cried the youngest kid, and she jumped inside the grandfather clock.

But the wolf was too quick for the other little kids. He chased them around the house and gobbled them all up!

"Yum, yum," said the wolf, patting his full tummy. He strolled out of the cottage and settled down for a nap under a nearby tree.

When Mother Goat came home she saw the door lying open.

She dropped her shopping basket and ran inside at once. "My darlings," she called "where are you?"

The youngest kid climbed out of the grandfather clock and into her mother's arms. "Mother, the wolf tricked us," she said. "He got into the house and gobbled everyone up!"

"I'm here now," soothed Mother Goat. "Let's go and teach that greedy old wolf a lesson."

"Look, Mother," said the youngest kid when they reached the end of their garden. "He's sleeping under that tree."

"I have a plan," whispered Mother Goat. "Fetch me some scissors and a needle and thread."

The youngest kid brought what she asked, and Mother Goat used her scissors to open the wolf's belly. The little kids jumped, one by one, out of the gap!

When all six were safely freed, they quickly filled the space left in the wolf's belly with large rocks, and Mother Goat sewed it back up with her needle and thread.

Hours later, Mother Goat and her little kids watched from the window as the wolf stood up and struggled away with his heavy belly.

Mother Goat and her little kids lived happily ever after, knowing the Big Bad Wolf would never be able to move fast enough to gobble up anyone else, ever again.

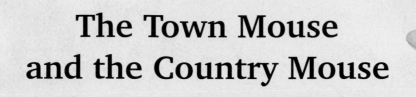

The Town Mouse
and the Country Mouse

Once upon a time, there were two little mice. One of them lived in the town, and the other one lived in the country.

One day, the Town Mouse decided that he would visit the Country Mouse. He had never been to the country before and he was very excited. He packed a small suitcase and went on his way.

Country Mouse's home was small and dark, not at all like Town Mouse's roomy home.

Lunch was very different, too. There was creamy cheese, juicy apples, and crispy, crunchy hazelnuts. It was all very tasty, but when Town Mouse had finished, he was still hungry.

After lunch, Country Mouse took Town Mouse for a walk. They went down a sunny path, through a creaky gate, and into a large field. Town Mouse was just starting to enjoy himself, when …

"Moo!"

"What was that?" he asked nervously, scurrying closer to Country Mouse.

"Ha! That's just a cow," said his friend. "There are lots of them in the country. It's nothing to be scared of."

Town Mouse and Country Mouse strolled on, through a flowery meadow and over a grassy hill. Soon, they came to a peaceful pond. Town Mouse was just starting to enjoy himself, when …

"Hiss!"

"What was that?" he asked again, trembling from nose to tail.

"Ha! That's just a goose," said his friend. "There are lots of them in the country. It's nothing to be scared of."

Town Mouse and Country Mouse kept on walking, across a rickety bridge, down a sandy track, and into a shady forest.

Town Mouse was just starting to enjoy himself, when …

"Twit-twoo!"

"What was that?" he yelped, pressing himself to the ground in terror.

"It's an owl!" cried Country Mouse. "Run for your life! If it catches you, it will eat you up!"

So the two mice ran and ran until they found a leafy hedge to hide in.

Town Mouse was terrified. "I don't like the country at all!" he said. "Come to stay with me in the town. You'll see how much better it is!"

Country Mouse had never been to the town before, so he packed a small bag and went to stay with his friend.

Town Mouse's home was huge and grand, not at all like Country Mouse's home.

Lunch was very different, too. Instead of apples and nuts, there were sandwiches and cupcakes. Lots and lots of them. It was tasty, but soon Country Mouse began to feel a bit sick. After dinner, the friends went out for a walk. They walked along pavements, past shops and offices. Country Mouse was just starting to enjoy himself, when …

"Beep-beep!"

"What's that?" he asked, looking about him.

"That? It's just a car," said his friend. "There are lots of them in the town. It's nothing to be afraid of."

Then the mice walked through a park, past a church, and down a wide road.

Country Mouse was just starting to enjoy himself, when …

"Nee-nah! Nee-nah!"

"What's that?" he asked again, his whiskers twitching.

"That? It's just a fire truck. There are lots of them in the town. It's nothing to be afraid of."

As the mice pitter-pattered home, they passed a school, some houses, and a pretty front yard. Country Mouse was just starting to enjoy himself, when …

"Meow!"

"What's that?" he squeaked, his eyes as wide as saucers.

"It's a cat!" cried Town Mouse. "Run for your life! If it catches you, it will eat you up!"

So the two mice ran and ran, all the way back to Town Mouse's home.

Country Mouse was terrified. "I don't like the town at all!" he said. "I'm going home to the country."

"But how can you be happy living near the cow and the goose and that horrible owl?" said Town Mouse.

"They don't scare me!" cried Country Mouse. "How can you be happy living near the cars and the fire trucks and that terrible cat?"

"They don't scare me!" cried Town Mouse.

The two mice looked at each other. Who was right and who was wrong? They would simply never agree.

So they shook hands and decided to go their separate ways: Town Mouse to his grand home and Country Mouse to his cozy one.

"Home, sweet home!" said the Town Mouse, sighing a deep, happy sigh.

"Home, sweet home!" said the Country Mouse, smiling a big, happy smile. And the two of them lived happily ever after, each in his own way.

The Dog and His Reflection

Puppy was having the best day of his life. The farmer had just given him his very first bone. It was a magnificent bone, with lots of juicy meat. Although Puppy couldn't wait to dig in, he wanted to show it off around the farm first.

"What a fine bone," said Hen as Puppy strutted proudly past.

"It's nearly as big as you!" laughed Cow.

"Mmm, that looks tasty," said Fox. "You wouldn't like to share it, would you?"

Puppy quickly trotted off, the bone still clenched firmly in his teeth. He was looking for a place where he could be on his own, with no one else hungrily watching him. So he headed for the woods.

Puppy had never been into the woods before. It always looked very dark and scary, but it seemed a good place to enjoy his bone in peace. But the woods were even scarier than he imagined. An owl hooted at him from the trees.

"Sorry, didn't mean to frighten you," said the owl. "I was just admiring your fine bone. Make sure you take good care of it."

Although the owl turned out to be friendly, Puppy still didn't really like the woods. So, he ran all the way through to the other side, where he found lush green fields.

Puppy had never been this far away from home. Soon he came to a wooden bridge over a clear river. This was very different from the streams around the farm, which were all muddy and full of weeds. Puppy was curious.

On the other side of the bridge, a family of rabbits was playing in the field.

"The rabbits won't want to share my bone," Puppy thought. "I'll dash over the river and dig into it in peace."

By now Puppy was feeling very hungry indeed. All he wanted was to sit in the soft grass and chew his bone in peace. He wobbled as he started crossing the old bridge. He tried not to look down, but when he reached the middle, he could not resist a quick glance.

He was surprised to see another dog peeping back.

Puppy went a bit closer to the edge to have a better look. As he did so, the other dog peeped out even farther so Puppy could now see his whole face. In between his teeth, he was also carrying a bone! And it looked just as big and juicy as Puppy's.

"I wish I could have that bone too," thought Puppy.

So, he started to growl at the other dog, hoping that it would make him drop the bone and run away.

Now the owl had flown out of the woods and come to perch on a nearby tree. He was watching Puppy very carefully.

"Oh dear," said the owl with a shake of his head.

Puppy began to growl even louder at the other dog. After all, that dog did not look any bigger than himself. But the other dog still refused to run off, seeming to growl back.

"It's not a real dog or a real bone," hooted the owl. "Be happy with what you already have instead of being greedy and trying to have even more."

But Puppy was not listening. He let out the fiercest bark he had ever made. **"Woof! Woof!"**

Immediately, the other dog dropped his bone.

Puppy felt very proud of himself. But then he realized that he didn't have his own bone either. It must have fallen out when he opened his mouth to bark. Yes, there it was—right at the bottom of the river!

Puppy sniffed miserably. He noticed that the other dog was sniffing miserably, too.

It was then that Puppy finally realized that the
other dog wasn't real at all. Nor was the bone. The owl
was right. It was just himself, reflected in the clear water.

Seeing what had happened, one of the little rabbits hopped
onto the bridge.

"Don't worry," he cried. "Come and play with us."

But Puppy did not feel like playing. Instead, feeling hungry
and sad, he set off on his own.

Just as the wise owl had told him, he should have been
content with the gift he had and not greedily wanted even more.

Chicken Little

One day, Chicken Little was walking in the woods when an acorn fell from a tree and bounced off his head. The acorn rolled away before Chicken Little knew what had hit him.

"Oh, my! Oh, dear!" he clucked. "The sky must be falling! Whatever shall I do?"

Chicken Little flew into a panic. He ran around in circles, losing feathers as he went.

He was still in a flap when his friend Henny Penny arrived.

"What's the matter?" she asked him.

"THE SKY IS FALLING! THE SKY IS FALLING!" cried Chicken Little.

Henny Penny was shocked. She did not know such a thing could happen. "Cluck-a-cluck-cluck!" she shrieked. "We must tell the king at once!"

So Chicken Little and Henny Penny rushed off to tell the king that the sky was falling. He'd know what to do.

They flapped down the road toward the palace, clucking as they went. Soon they met Cocky Locky.

"Where are you going in such a hurry?" he asked.

"THE SKY IS FALLING! THE SKY IS FALLING!" Chicken Little cried at once.

"And we're off to tell the king!" chattered Henny Penny.

Cocky Locky gasped. It would be terrible if the sky fell. "Cock-a-doodle-doo," he crowed. "I'll come with you!"

So Chicken Little, Henny Penny, and Cocky Locky rushed off to tell the king that the sky was falling.

They flapped and they flustered down the road to the palace, clucking and crowing as they went. Soon they met Ducky Lucky.

"Why are you flapping so?" she asked. **"THE SKY IS FALLING! THE SKY IS FALLING!"** cried Chicken Little.

"We're off to tell the king!" crowed Cocky Locky.

Ducky Lucky frowned. She didn't like the sound of the sky falling at all. "How w-w-worrying," she quacked nervously. "I'm c-c-coming with you."

So Chicken Little, Henny Penny, Cocky Locky, and Ducky Lucky rushed off together to tell the king that the sky was falling.

They flapped and they flustered and they fidgeted down the road to the palace, clucking and crowing and quacking as they went. Soon they met Drakey Lakey.

"What's all the fuss about?" he asked.

"THE SKY IS FALLING! THE SKY IS FALLING!" cried Chicken Little.

"We're off to tell the king!" quacked Ducky Lucky.

Drakey Lakey was dumbfounded. He dreaded the thought of a falling sky. "Darn it!" he squawked. "I'll join you on your journey!"

So Chicken Little, Henny Penny, Cocky Locky, Ducky Lucky, and Drakey Lakey rushed off to tell the king that the sky was falling.

They flapped and they flustered and they fidgeted and they flurried down the road to the palace, clucking and crowing and quacking and squawking as they went. Soon they met Goosey Loosey.

"What's ruffled your feathers?" she asked.

"THE SKY IS FALLING! THE SKY IS FALLING!" cried Chicken Little.

"We're off to tell the king!" squawked Drakey Lakey.

140

Goosey Loosey shuddered. Could it really be true? "How horrible!" she honked. "I'm coming with you."

So Chicken Little, Henny Penny, Cocky Locky, Ducky Lucky, Drakey Lakey, and Goosey Loosey rushed off to tell the king that the sky was falling.

They flapped and they flustered and they fidgeted and they flurried and they flopped down the road to the palace, clucking and crowing and quacking and squawking and honking as they went. Soon they met Turkey Lurkey.

"Where are you waddling to?" she asked.

"THE SKY IS FALLING! THE SKY IS FALLING!" cried Chicken Little.

"We're off to tell the king!" honked Goosey Loosey.

Turkey Lurkey trembled. She thought that sounded truly terrible!

141

"My goodness!" she gobbled. "I'm coming with you!"

So Chicken Little, Henny Penny, Cocky Locky, Ducky Lucky, Drakey Lakey, Goosey Loosey, and Turkey Lurkey rushed off to tell the king that the sky was falling.

They flapped and they flustered and they fidgeted and they flurried and they flopped and they floundered down the road to the palace, clucking and crowing and quacking and squawking and honking and gobbling as they went. Soon they met Foxy Loxy.

"Well, hello!" he said. "Why are you all in such a tizzy?"

"THE SKY IS FALLING! THE SKY IS FALLING!" cried Chicken Little.

"We're off to tell the king!" gobbled Turkey Lurkey.

Foxy Loxy smiled slyly. He had never seen so many plump birds in such a fearsome flap.

"Well I never," soothed Foxy Loxy. "Don't worry, I know the quickest way to reach the king. Follow me."

So Chicken Little, Henny Penny, Cocky Locky, Ducky Lucky, Drakey Lakey, Goosey Loosey, and Turkey Lurkey followed Foxy Loxy down a long path and into some dark woods.

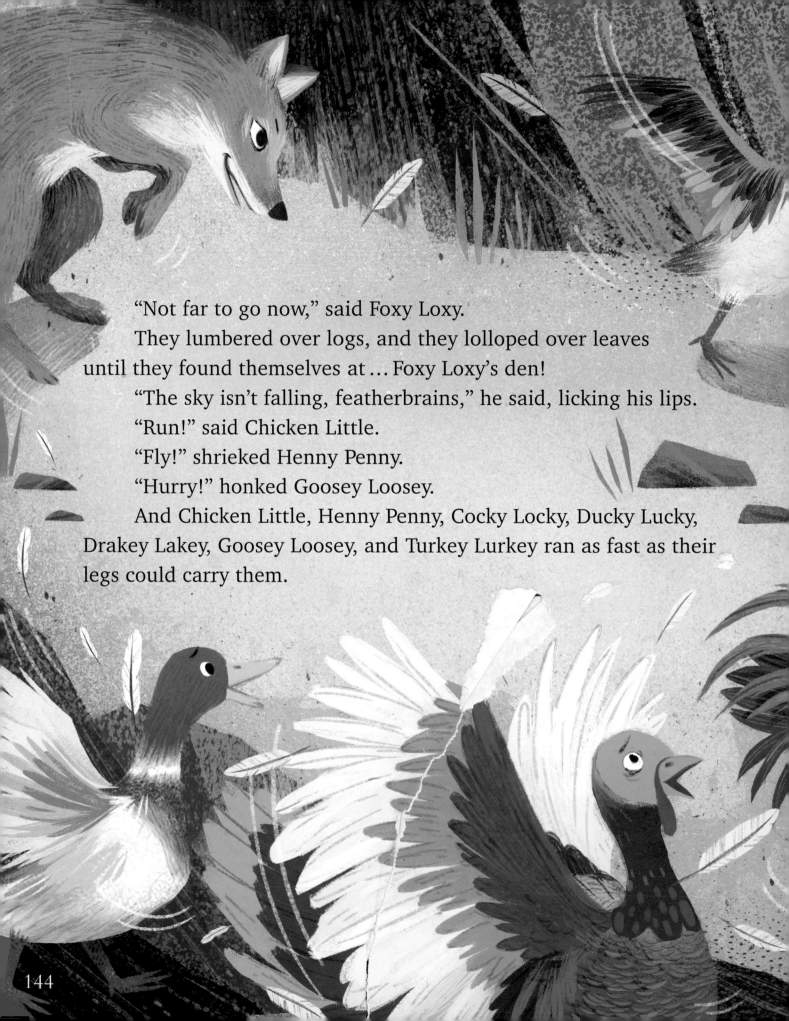

"Not far to go now," said Foxy Loxy.

They lumbered over logs, and they lolloped over leaves until they found themselves at ... Foxy Loxy's den!

"The sky isn't falling, featherbrains," he said, licking his lips.

"Run!" said Chicken Little.

"Fly!" shrieked Henny Penny.

"Hurry!" honked Goosey Loosey.

And Chicken Little, Henny Penny, Cocky Locky, Ducky Lucky, Drakey Lakey, Goosey Loosey, and Turkey Lurkey ran as fast as their legs could carry them.

They flapped and they flustered,
and they fidgeted and they flurried,
and they flopped and they floundered, right out of the woods
and back up the long path, clucking and crowing and quacking
and squawking and honking and gobbling as they went.

When at last they were safe, Chicken Little looked up at the
sky. It was still there!

Maybe it really hadn't been falling after all…

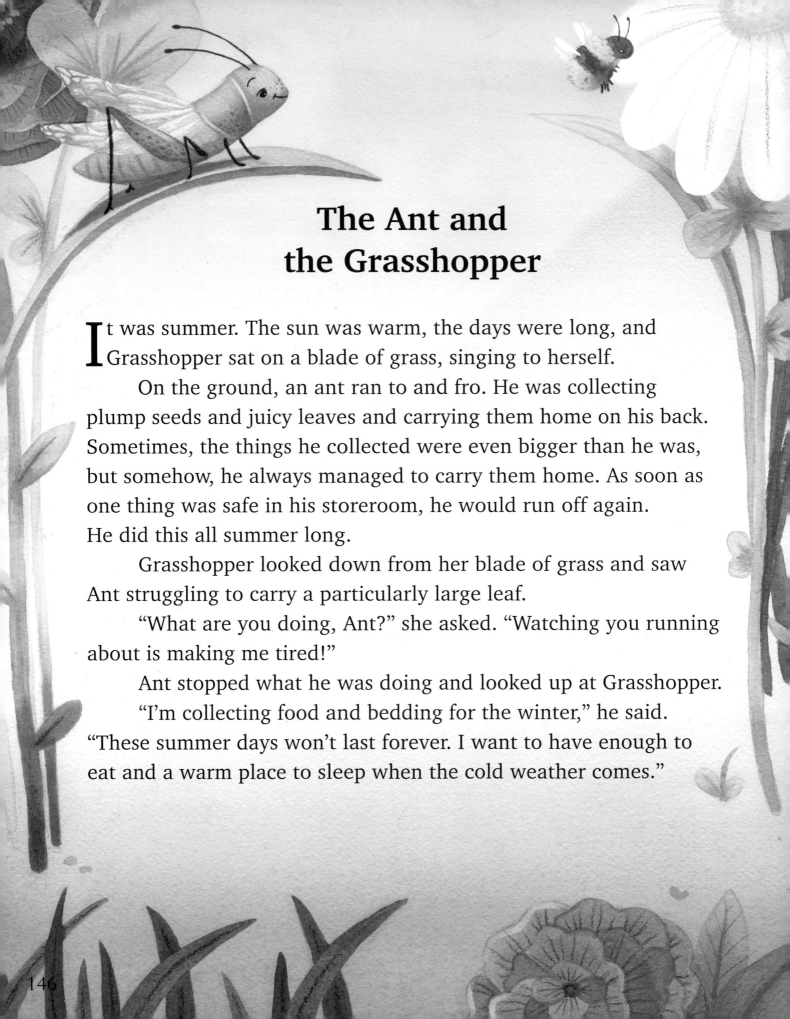

The Ant and
the Grasshopper

It was summer. The sun was warm, the days were long, and Grasshopper sat on a blade of grass, singing to herself.

On the ground, an ant ran to and fro. He was collecting plump seeds and juicy leaves and carrying them home on his back. Sometimes, the things he collected were even bigger than he was, but somehow, he always managed to carry them home. As soon as one thing was safe in his storeroom, he would run off again. He did this all summer long.

Grasshopper looked down from her blade of grass and saw Ant struggling to carry a particularly large leaf.

"What are you doing, Ant?" she asked. "Watching you running about is making me tired!"

Ant stopped what he was doing and looked up at Grasshopper.

"I'm collecting food and bedding for the winter," he said. "These summer days won't last forever. I want to have enough to eat and a warm place to sleep when the cold weather comes."

Grasshopper wrinkled her nose. "What a waste of time! While you're working, you're missing the sun on your back and the breeze through the grass. I just can't bear thinking about winter when there's so much summer to enjoy."

"Please yourself," said Ant, "but if you'll excuse me, I must be off. I have a lot of work to do." With that, he picked up the leaf again and disappeared into the undergrowth.

It seemed that summer would last forever. Grasshopper continued to spend her days relaxing in the sun, singing her songs, and chattering with the bees.

"Poor Ant," she said to herself. "What a shame to work so hard and miss all this fun."

Then one morning, the weather changed. The sun still shone, but it was no longer warm. The leaves on the apple trees were yellow, and a cold wind whirled them through the air. The grass tips were white with frost. The birds flew off to warmer lands, and the bees would no longer stay and chat with Grasshopper. It was fall.

Grasshopper began to worry that maybe she should be rushing off somewhere, too, but she didn't know where.

Time went by, and fall turned to winter. The days were short, and the sun never shone. Frost clung to every stem and stone. The bees had disappeared, and Grasshopper shivered alone on her blade of grass because she had nowhere warm to go.

"I have no food or shelter. How can I survive in the cold?" she whimpered. "I must try to find somewhere out of this wind." She crawled down the grass and buried herself in the leaves on the ground to sleep. The sky grew darker, and the wind howled.

Ant was hurrying home through the undergrowth when he happened to see her half-hidden in the leaves.

"Silly Grasshopper!" Ant thought to himself. "You did nothing but sing and sunbathe all summer, and now look at you." But he was a kind ant, so he took pity on the poor frozen creature.

"Wake up, Grasshopper!" he whispered gently. "You can't stay here any longer in this cold. Let me take you somewhere warm."

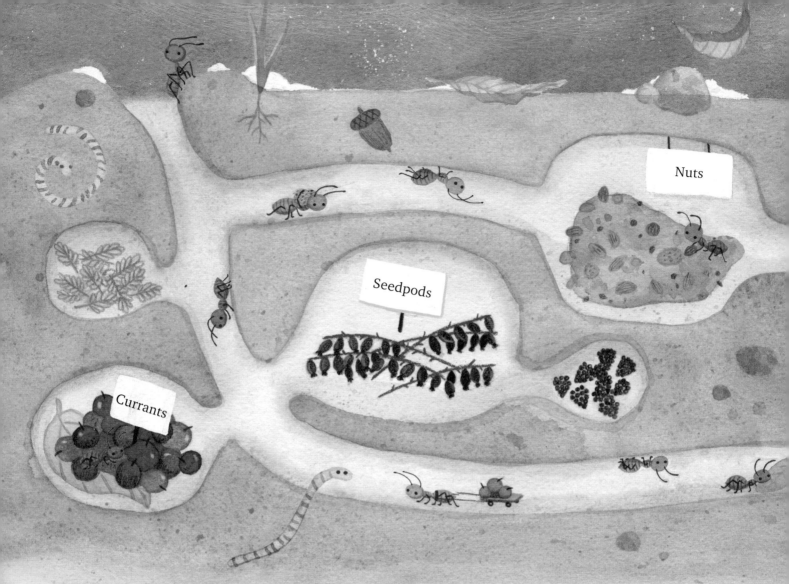

Nuts

Seedpods

Currants

Grasshopper opened her eyes, but she was too weak to move, so Ant carried her all the way to his home and then down through tunnels deep in the earth. It was warmer down there, and at last, Grasshopper began to feel better.

Looking around to her left and her right, she could see storerooms full of the seeds and leaves that Ant had collected during the summer. Ant had worked very hard indeed, thought Grasshopper miserably.

Grain

Berries

Leaves

At last, Ant and Grasshopper reached the end of the tunnel, where there was a large cozy bedroom, with a soft, warm bed.

"Now, Grasshopper, lie down here and rest," said Ant kindly. "You had better stay with me this winter."

"Oh, thank you," said Grasshopper, tearfully. "You have saved my life. I was such a fool, wasting all those summer days. I should have been working hard like you, and then I wouldn't be in this trouble. Next year, I'll work all through the summer, I promise."

The Rooster
and the Fox

There once was a wise old rooster who lived on a farm with ten plump hens. Every day, as the sun rose, the rooster flew up to sit on a branch in a tall tree beside the farmyard gate. He could see the whole farm and the countryside around it. Once he had checked that all was safe, the rooster would take a deep breath, puff out his chest, and give an almighty **COCK-A-DOODLE-DOO**. This woke the hens and let them know that it was safe for them to come out into the yard. They had nothing to fear.

One morning, a fox was trotting past the farm, when he saw the rooster high up in the tree. The fox was hungry, and the rooster was plump and well fed—just the sort of tasty meal the fox was looking for. If he could lure the rooster to fly down from the tree, thought the fox, he could eat him for breakfast. And once he was gone, there would be no one to protect the hens, so the fox could eat them up, too.

With this in mind, the fox trotted up to the gate. He knew he would have to be clever to trick the rooster, but he had a plan.

"Good morning," he said politely, looking up at the rooster. "Have you heard the good news?"

The rooster looked down at the fox. He knew that the fox was cunning, so he guessed that this was some kind of trick.

"No," he said cautiously. "What good news are you talking about?"

The fox smiled knowingly. "The king has announced that all the animals and birds in the land must be friends," said the fox. "It's forbidden for them to eat each other. Isn't that wonderful? Come down out of your tree, and I'll tell you more about it."

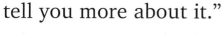

The rooster tipped his head to one side.

"Is that so?" he said. "I'm very pleased to hear it. So if I came down out of this tree and spoke to you, you wouldn't jump on me and eat me up?"

"Oh, no," said the fox sweetly. "That would be completely against the law. Please come down so that we can be friends."

The rooster looked out over the countryside. Then he blinked and blinked again, as if he had seen something very interesting in the far distance.

"What are you looking at?" asked the fox, who was feeling hungrier every minute.

"I can see a pack of dogs running through the forest," said the rooster. "They're running very fast, and they seem to be coming this way."

"Goodness, how time flies!" said the fox nervously. "I've just remembered that I'm late for an appointment. Please excuse me, Rooster, I have to go at once."

"Oh, please don't go," said the rooster. "I'm coming down right now. I want you to tell me all about the wonderful announcement. The dogs will be here soon, too, and we can all discuss it together, now that there's nothing for you to fear."

"Oh, no," said the fox, now shaking with fear. "I really must go. Those dogs don't know about the announcement yet, so I'm afraid they will eat me."

With that, the fox ran off and disappeared across the fields on the other side of the farm.

The rooster watched him go from his seat in the tree. Then he puffed out his chest and gave the most almighty **COCK-A-DOODLE-DOO!** It was safe once again for the hens to come out into the yard.

The Vain Crow

There was once a young crow who loved to talk about himself. Every day he marched up and down the branches of a tall tree.

"I'm the most beautiful crow," he said to the other crows in the tree. "I have the smoothest feathers and the loudest voice. I am the best bird in the world!"

"We're all the same," said the other crows. "You're just a vain crow."

"Nonsense," said the vain crow. "I'm prettier than all of you."

One day, as he was flying over the king's garden, the vain crow saw a group of beautiful peacocks.

"Look at my gorgeous feathers," said one, fanning out his glorious tail.

"You look wonderful," said his friend, stretching out his wings so they sparkled in the sun. The vain crow hid behind some flowers to watch them.

"I belong with these birds," he said to a passing mouse. "I am just as beautiful as they are."

"But their feathers are glorious and yours aren't," said the mouse.

"My feathers are special!" replied the vain crow. "Look closer."

"They're shiny and neat," said the mouse. "But they're not as magnificent as the peacocks'."

The vain crow knew the mouse was right. He turned to fly home, but just then a peacock passed nearby ... and a few of his colorful tail feathers dropped onto the grass!

Quick as a flash, the vain crow scooped the feathers up. He flew back to his tree, found some sticky sap, and carefully glued the feathers to his own tail.

"I'm going to live with the peacocks," he said to the crows. "I need to be around birds who will recognize my beauty."

When the vain crow arrived back in the garden, he landed on a tall rock. "Look at me, peacocks!" he called, waggling his tail feathers at them. "I'm a rare and beautiful new bird, and I've come to take my rightful place in the king's garden."

The peacocks were curious about this exotic creature, but as they came closer one of them noticed the sticky sap on the vain crow's tail. "You're just a crow!" he said.

The peacocks plucked each colorful feather out of the vain crow's tail. "We don't want to be friends with a vain bird who doesn't tell the truth," they said.

The peacocks turned their beautiful tails on the vain crow and stalked away.

The vain crow felt so silly that he flew back to his tree as fast as he could.

"Those peacocks are not so beautiful close up," he said. "I'll stay here, as the most beautiful bird in the tree."

"We don't want to be friends with such a vain crow," said the other crows. "Go away."

"But wait," said the vain crow. "Who will I talk to?"

"You can talk to yourself," they replied. With that, they flew away to roost in a nearby tree.

The vain crow wrapped his wings around himself, feeling miserable and lonely.

"Those mean peacocks didn't want me, and now my old friends the crows have flown away," he thought. "If only I hadn't been so vain, or tried to be something I'm not."

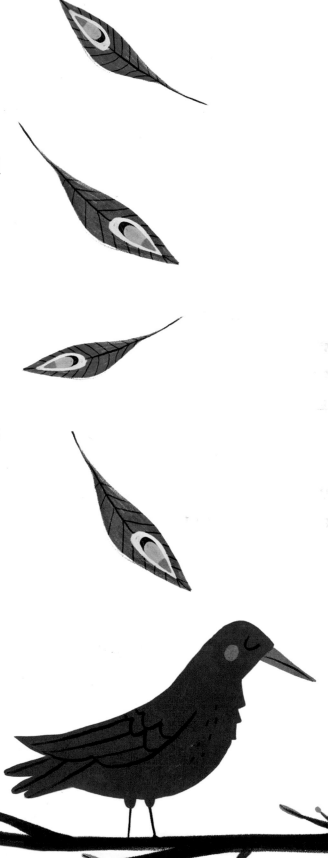

Songs and Rhymes

Old Mother Goose

Old Mother Goose,
When she wanted to wander,
Would ride through the air
On a very fine gander.

Mother Goose had a house,
It stood in the wood,
Where an owl at the door
As a sentinel stood.

She had a son, Jack,
A plain looking lad.
He was not very good,
Nor yet very bad.

She sent him to market,
A live goose he bought.
"See, Mother," he said,
"I have not been for naught."

Jack's goose and her gander,
Soon grew very fond.
They'd both eat together,
Or swim in the pond.

Then, one finé morning,
As I have been told,
Jack's goose had laid him
An egg of pure gold.

Itsy Bitsy Spider

The itsy bitsy spider climbed up the water spout.
Down came the rain,
And washed the spider out.
Out came the sun
And dried up all the rain,
And the itsy bitsy spider
Climbed up the spout again.

Ride a Cock-Horse

Ride a cock-horse to Banbury Cross,
To see a fine lady upon a white horse.
With rings on her fingers and bells on her toes,
She shall have music wherever she goes.

Five Little Ducks

Five little ducks went swimming one day,
Over the pond and far away.
Mother duck said, "Quack, quack, quack!"
But only four little ducks came back.

Four little ducks went swimming one day,
Over the pond and far away.
Mother duck said, "Quack, quack, quack!"
But only three little ducks came back.

Three little ducks went swimming one day,
Over the pond and far away.
Mother duck said, "Quack, quack, quack!"
But only two little ducks came back.

Two little ducks went swimming one day,
Over the pond and far away.
Mother duck said, "Quack, quack, quack!"
But only one little duck came back.

One little duck went swimming one day,
Over the pond and far away.
Mother duck said, "Quack, quack, quack!"
But no little ducks came swimming back.

No little ducks went swimming one day,
Over the pond and far away.
Mother duck said, "Quack, quack, quack!"
And five little ducks came swimming back.

Sing a Song of Sixpence

Sing a song of sixpence,
A pocket full of rye;
Four and twenty blackbirds
Baked in a pie.
When the pie was opened,
The birds began to sing;
Now wasn't that a dainty dish
To set before the king?

The king was in his counting house,
Counting out his money;
The queen was in the parlor,
Eating bread and honey.
The maid was in the garden,
Hanging out the clothes,
When down came a blackbird
And pecked off her nose!

The Animals
Went in Two by Two

The animals went in two by two
Hoorah! Hoorah!
The animals went in two by two
Hoorah! Hoorah!

The animals went in two by two
The elephant and the kangaroo
And they all went into the ark
To get out of the rain.

The animals went in three by three
Hoorah! Hoorah!
The animals went in three by three
Hoorah! Hoorah!

The animals went in three by three
The wasp, the ant and the bumblebee
And they all went into the ark
To get out of the rain.

The animals went in four by four
Hoorah! Hoorah!
The animals went in four by four
Hoorah! Hoorah!

The animals went in four by four
The great hippopotamus stuck in the door
And they all went into the ark
To get out of the rain.

The animals went in five by five
Hoorah! Hoorah!
The animals went in five by five
Hoorah! Hoorah!

The animals went in five by five
By hugging each other they kept alive
And they all went into the ark
To get out of the rain.

The animals went in six by six
Hoorah! Hoorah!
The animals went in six by six
Hoorah! Hoorah!

The animals went in six by six
They turned out the monkey because of his tricks
And they all went into the ark
To get out of the rain.

The animals went in seven by seven
Hoorah! Hoorah!
The animals went in seven by seven
Hoorah! Hoorah!

The animals went in seven by seven
The little pig thought he was going to heaven
And they all went into the ark
To get out of the rain.

The animals went in eight by eight
Hoorah! Hoorah!
The animals went in eight by eight
Hoorah! Hoorah!

The animals went in eight by eight
The tortoise thought he was going to be late
And they all went into the ark
To get out of the rain.

The animals went in nine by nine
Hoorah! Hoorah!
The animals went in nine by nine
Hoorah! Hoorah!

The animals went in nine by nine
Marching up in a long straight line
And they all went into the ark
To get out of the rain.

The animals went in ten by ten
Hoorah! Hoorah!
The animals went in ten by ten
Hoorah! Hoorah!

The animals went in ten by ten
The last one in was the little red hen
And they all went into the ark
To get out of the rain.

B-I-N-G-O

There was a farmer had a dog,
And Bingo was his name-o.
    B-I-N-G-O
    B-I-N-G-O
    B-I-N-G-O
And Bingo was his name-o.

There was a farmer had a dog,
And Bingo was his name-o.
    (clap)-I-N-G-O
    (clap)-I-N-G-O
    (clap)-I-N-G-O
And Bingo was his name-o.

There was a farmer had a dog,
And Bingo was his name-o.
    (clap)-(clap)-N-G-O
    (clap)-(clap)-N-G-O
    (clap)-(clap)-N-G-O
And Bingo was his name-o.

There was a farmer had a dog,
And Bingo was his name-o.
(clap)-(clap)-(clap)-G-O
(clap)-(clap)-(clap)-G-O
(clap)-(clap)-(clap)-G-O
And Bingo was his name-o.

There was a farmer had a dog,
And Bingo was his name-o.
(clap)-(clap)-(clap)-(clap)-O
(clap)-(clap)-(clap)-(clap)-O
(clap)-(clap)-(clap)-(clap)-O
And Bingo was his name-o.

There was a farmer had a dog,
And Bingo was his name-o.
(clap)-(clap)-(clap)-(clap)-(clap)
(clap)-(clap)-(clap)-(clap)-(clap)
(clap)-(clap)-(clap)-(clap)-(clap)
And Bingo was his name-o.

This Little Piggy

This little piggy went to market,
And this little piggy stayed at home,
This little piggy had roast beef,
And this little piggy had none,
And this little piggy cried,
"Wee, wee, wee, wee, wee!"
All the way home.

Hickety Pickety

Hickety Pickety, my black hen,
She lays eggs for gentlemen;
Sometimes nine, and sometimes ten,
Hickety Pickety, my black hen!

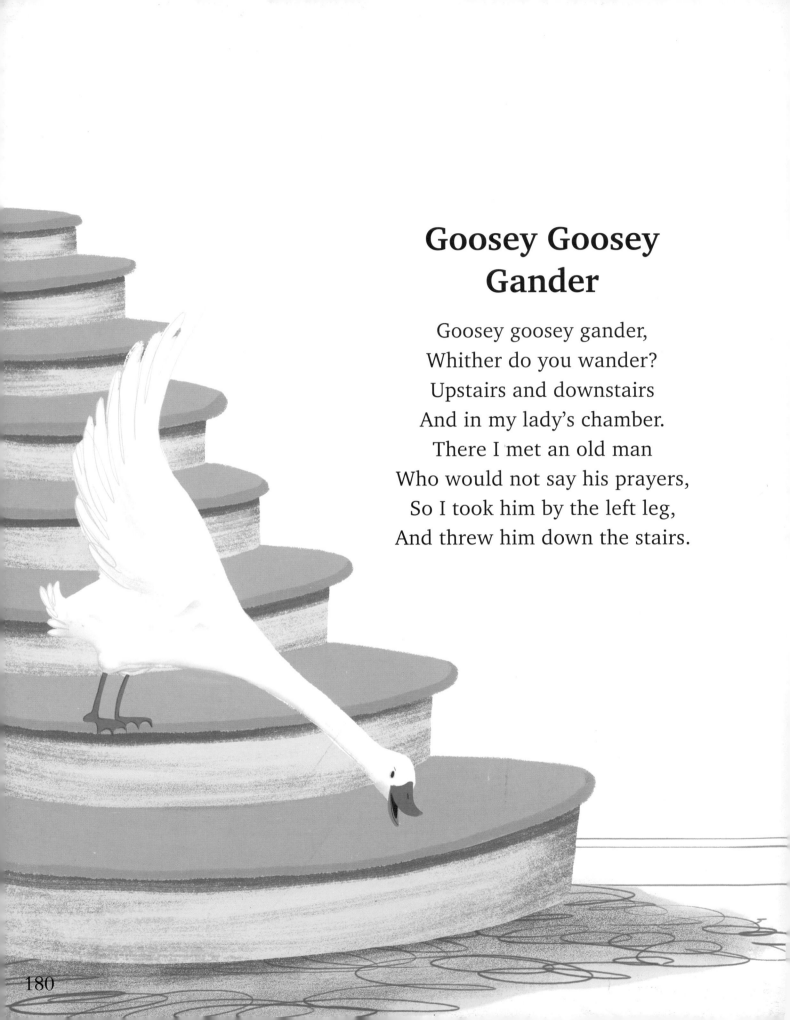

Goosey Goosey Gander

Goosey goosey gander,
Whither do you wander?
Upstairs and downstairs
And in my lady's chamber.
There I met an old man
Who would not say his prayers,
So I took him by the left leg,
And threw him down the stairs.

Baa, Baa, Black Sheep

"Baa, baa, black sheep,
Have you any wool?"
"Yes, sir, yes, sir,
Three bags full;
One for the master,
And one for the dame,
And one for the little boy
Who lives down the lane."

Mary Had a Little Lamb

Mary had a little lamb,
Whose fleece was white as snow.
And everywhere that Mary went
The lamb was sure to go.

It followed her to school one day,
Which was against the rules,
It made the children laugh and play,
To see a lamb at school.

And so the teacher turned it out,
But still it lingered near,
It waited patiently about,
Till Mary did appear.

"Why does the lamb love Mary so?"
The eager children cried.
"Why, Mary loves the lamb, you know,"
The teacher did reply.

Hey Diddle Diddle

Hey diddle diddle,
The cat and the fiddle,
The cow jumped over the moon.

The little dog laughed,
To see such fun,
And the dish ran away with the spoon.

Little Bo-Peep

Little Bo-Peep has lost her sheep,
And doesn't know where to find them;
Leave them alone,
And they'll come home,
Wagging their tails behind them.

Pussycat, Pussycat

"Pussycat, pussycat,
Where have you been?"
"I've been to London
To visit the Queen."
"Pussycat, pussycat,
What did you there?"
"I frightened a little mouse
Under her chair."

Old MacDonald
Had a Farm

Old MacDonald had a farm,
E-I-E-I-O.
And on that farm he had some cows,
E-I-E-I-O.
With a **moo moo** here and a **moo moo** there,
Here a **moo**, there a **moo**,
Everywhere a **moo moo**.
Old MacDonald had a farm,
E-I-E-I-O.

Old MacDonald had a farm,
E-I-E-I-O.
And on that farm he had some ducks,
E-I-E-I-O.
With a **quack quack** here and a **quack quack** there,
Here a **quack**, there a **quack**,
Everywhere a **quack quack**.
Old MacDonald had a farm,
E-I-E-I-O.

Old MacDonald had a farm,
E-I-E-I-O.
And on that farm he had some sheep,
E-I-E-I-O.
With a **baa baa** here and a **baa baa** there,
Here a **baa**, there a **baa**,
Everywhere a **baa baa**.
Old MacDonald had a farm,
E-I-E-I-O.

Old MacDonald had a farm,
E-I-E-I-O.
And on that farm he had some dogs,
E-I-E-I-O.
With a **woof woof** here and a **woof woof** there,
Here a **woof**, there a **woof**,
Everywhere a **woof woof**.
Old MacDonald had a farm,
E-I-E-I-O.

The
end